The Adventures of Boone Barnaby

Other Apple Paperbacks
you will enjoy:

Shoebag
by Mary James

The Two-Thousand-Pound Goldfish
by Betsy Byars

Afternoon of the Elves
by Janet Taylor Lisle

Family Picture
by Dean Hughes

Home Sweet Home, Good-bye
by Cynthia Stowe

Oh, Brother
by Johnniece Marshall Wilson

The Adventures of Boone Barnaby

Joe Cottonwood

SCHOLASTIC INC.
New York Toronto London Auckland Sydney

ISBN 0-590-43547-7

12 11 10 9 8 7 6 5 4 3 2 1   11   2 3 4 5 6 7/9

Printed in the U.S.A.   28

Contents

The Adventures of Boone Barnaby

1.
Babcock

I live in San Puerco, California. It's a little town in the Santa Cruz Mountains. There are just a few people and a whole mess of big trees tall enough to trap the fog blowing in from the Pacific Ocean. It's so quiet here, ducks sleep on the street. Banana slugs suck on our windows. Just about everybody has a wood stove and a pickup truck — except my dad. He has a computer and a Volkswagen bus.

The day after Labor Day, the morning of the first day of the new school year, I had just one thought on my mind: *soccer*. We had a team; we had a coach, an assistant coach, a league to play in; but we only had ten players. First day of school, I might find a new kid, a speedy kid, a strong kid who could run like lightning and kick like thunder. Our team is *The San Puerco Thunderbolts*. Last year, we never won a game. We were always playing ten against eleven. My dad said maybe we should pick a new name: *The San Puerco Doormats*. He was joking.

If there was a new kid in town I'd probably already know it, but as my dad says, you never can tell who — or what — is going to come out of the woods. And we have a lot of woods. Redwoods.

First thing I saw in the schoolyard was Danny with a wicked grin on his face. "Guess what I found," he said.

"A Thunderbolt? Number eleven?"

"Nope," said Danny. "Not a Thunderbolt. A raindrop, maybe. Round and soft and wet. And when it hits the ground, it goes *plop*." Again he grinned.

"Who?"

"Him." Danny pointed across the playground where I saw a new kid, a fat kid carrying a briefcase. The fat kid was black.

Danny's brown. I'm white. And that's about all there is to say about color. It's never been an issue with Danny or me.

"Aw, Danny," I said.

"Come on, Boone," said Danny, still grinning. "Let's have some *fun*."

Sometimes Danny thinks it's fun to step on worms or throw stones at squirrels. When he gets that way, I tag along so I can try to stop him. I could just leave, but he's my friend and my soccer buddy. He's like a half-trained puppy tearing into a shoe — you can't teach him not to chew, but you can try to interest him in something he's allowed to have, like a bone.

Danny was sauntering across the asphalt around some girls skipping rope. I followed. I made up my mind to keep my mouth shut and my hands in my pockets, at least until I could find out what he had in mind.

The fat kid was kneeling over some pebbles next to a garden where a couple of straggly red flowers were blooming. He picked up a shiny white rock and rubbed it between his fingers.

"What's that?" Danny said.

"A pebble," said the fat kid, looking up.

"Dsh," said Danny, which is something he says a lot. It rhymes with bush, sort of, only with more *sh* and no middle, and what it means is — well, it can mean anything. In this case, it meant "*Duh*. Of course. Tell me something I don't already know."

But the fat kid didn't know what it meant. He only stared at Danny, looking slightly nervous as if he knew what Danny was leading up to and had been through it many times before on many other first days of school.

"Dsh dsh," said Danny.

"*What?*" said the fat kid.

"The pebble," said Danny, grinning. "A gold nugget?"

The fat kid stood up. "Quartz," he said. "Milky quartz." He opened his briefcase — *sproing* went the latches — and dropped the pebble inside.

"You collect quartz?" asked Danny.

The fat kid pulled a blue handkerchief out of his back pocket and wiped his forehead and upper lip. He was sweating. "I collect everything under the sun," he said.

"Dsh," said Danny, nodding. I know what he meant: *Nobody* at our school carried a briefcase, and nobody in the whole *world* who we had ever met carried a handkerchief in his pocket. Then Danny, grinning again, said, "You collect candy bars? Doughnuts? Pecan pies?"

"All right." The fat kid suddenly smiled. He didn't relax, but he smiled. He looked as if he knew exactly what Danny was up to now, and though he may not have liked it, at least he was ready for it.

Danny stopped grinning. He hadn't expected the kid to *smile* at him. "Dsh," he said, which I think meant he didn't know what else to say.

"Look. I'm the fat kid," said the fat kid. "And you must be the bully."

Danny stepped forward. "I ain't no bully," he said. "Sorry."

"Take it back!"

"Is that an order?"

"Yes!"

The fat kid looked at me. I still had my hands in my pockets. "Danny," I said. "Ease up." I couldn't think of any bone to throw him.

Danny wouldn't back down. He was right in the fat kid's face. "You called me a name," he said. "Take it back."

The fat kid sighed. He shrugged. He set down his briefcase. "No," he said.

Danny pushed him in the chest.

The fat kid didn't budge. Danny, in fact, stepped backward as if he'd pushed off against a wall. He stepped up again. He was making fists.

Again, strangely, the fat kid smiled.

Danny hit him in the belly. The fat kid said, "Oof," but then he made a move like falling on his side while rolling out his legs, which caught Danny at the ankles and tripped him to the ground. Quicker than I would've thought a fat kid could move, he was sitting on top of Danny in the garden between two ragged flower stalks.

Danny couldn't even wiggle. About a dozen kids were standing in a half circle around us. "Lemme out," Danny squeaked. "I can't *breathe*."

The fat kid stood up and brushed off his pants. "Sorry," he said.

"Dsh," said Danny. "What's your name?"

"Babcock."

"What's your first name?"

"Babcock."

"Well, then, what's your *last* name?"

"Babcock."

"Babcock Babcock?" Danny shook his head. "Dsh."

"No. Just Babcock. That's all."

"But you gotta have more than one name."

"Says who?"

Danny shrugged. "Dsh," he said.

"And what's *your* name?" said Babcock. "Dsh?"

"No. Danny." He smiled. "And this is my buddy Boone," he said, pointing at me.

"Hello, Boone. Buddy Boone. Hello, Danny Dsh."

"Hello, Babcock," I said.

"Dsh," said Danny. Then he grinned. "Hey Babcock," he said. "You play soccer?"

"No."

"Wanna try?"

Babcock smiled, and this time it was real.

When the bell rang, the principal came out and read the names of who belonged in what classroom. Danny, Babcock, and I were in the same class, which was no surprise. There's only one teacher for each grade at my school, and some grades have to double up. As my dad says, "Small town, small school, small minds." But I don't think he means it about the minds.

Our teacher was Mrs. Rule. Everybody knew she was strict but fair. She had taut black skin and flashing eyes. She kept her hair in a bun with not one hair hanging free. Her clothes never wrinkled. I never saw her sweat. Danny said once, "I bet her *caca* don't even stink."

Mrs. Rule called the roll. "Elizabeth Abrams?"

"Here."

"Susanna Ardale?"

"Here."

"Babcock?"

"Here."

A giggle ran through the girls in the class.

Mrs. Rule shot them The Look. Immediately, they were silent. She had one of those looks that could split boulders.

"Mr. Babcock has only one name," she said to the class. "We will have to get used to that." She turned to Babcock. "Would you like to explain why you only have one name?"

"No," said Babcock.

"Do you mind if I expla — "

"Yes," said Babcock.

"Hmm," said Mrs. Rule. She gave Babcock the same look she'd given the giggling girls.

Babcock met her eye. He had the same unrelaxed smile on his face that I'd seen him give Danny just before the fight.

Not a sound in the room.

Mrs. Rule clucked her tongue. I suppose it was like Danny saying dsh. It could mean anything.

I saw sweat gathering on Babcock's upper lip.

Then, to my surprise, Mrs. Rule looked down at her attendance list. "Boone Barnaby?" she said.

"Here," I said.

Score one, I thought, for Babcock.

Babcock came to soccer practice wearing the same clothes he'd worn to school. His pants were already dirty from the scuffle he'd had with Danny. Everybody else on the team was wearing shorts, cleats, and shin-guards.

"You got any shorts?" Danny asked.

"No," Babcock said.

"Dsh. You'll need some."

"Why?"

"For soccer. Everybody wears shorts."

"Why?"

"Because," Danny said, "you get *hot*."

"Not me," Babcock said, wiping his forehead with a handkerchief.

The first thing at practice, the coach always tells us to take a lap. We run in a bunch except for Dylan, who always falls behind — sometimes, *way* behind if he gets distracted by a lizard or a bumblebee. Dylan is the coach's son. It's not that he's slow. He's like a butterfly. You never know what flower he'll light on next.

The coach arrived, late, and immediately said, "OK, team, take a lap."

"What?" said Babcock.

"A lap," the coach said. "Who are you?"

I said, "This is Babcock. He wants to join the team."

"Do you?" the coach said.

"Well, sir, Danny said you needed another player. I thought I'd try it out."

The coach looked him up and down, from sweating forehead to fat body to long pants to leather shoes. Babcock was still holding his briefcase.

The coach shook his head. "You try us out," he said. "And we'll try *you* out. Now, take a lap."

"Lap what?" Babcock said.

"Run," I said. "Around the field."

Babcock groaned. But he set down the briefcase and started to jog. His cheeks bounced as he ran.

We ran in a bunch with Dylan slightly behind and Babcock way back, looking like he was going to die. Then as I kept on running I saw Dylan stop, reach down, and pick something up. He stood there, examining it, as Babcock lumbered up to him. Babcock stopped. He studied the item in Dylan's hand. Then they both set off jogging, slowly, at Babcock's pace, talking and looking at whatever was in Dylan's hand.

We milled around and kicked some balls. The coach, whose name is Walt, paced back and forth. Walt has a white beard and looks about a hundred years old, but he says he's forty something. He rides around on a big, black Harley Davidson motorcycle.

When Dylan and Babcock finally arrived three minutes later, Walt said sarcastically, "Thank you for joining us again."

Babcock wiped his face with a blue handkerchief.

Dylan said, "We found a dead dragonfly."

"Damselfly," Babcock said.

"Dragonfly," Dylan said.

"Babcock," Walt said, "I would say that speed is not your greatest asset. Would you agree with that?"

"Depends, sir. Slow, yes. I'm quick, though."

Walt frowned. "You're slow. But you're quick." He

shook his head. "I suppose you're also stupid. But smart."

"My father would probably say so, sir."

"Let's try you at goalie."

"Hurray!" Dylan shouted. He'd been our goalie, and hated it.

"Yes, sir," Babcock said.

"Call me Walt."

"Yes, sir."

"Get in the goal, and we'll try some shots."

"Yes, sir," Babcock said. He looked around the field. He didn't move. "What's the goal?"

Walt turned his face to the sky. "Great galloping banana slugs!" he said to the clouds. "Why me?"

Jack was just arriving. Jack is a hotshot high school soccer player who helps Walt as assistant coach.

"Jack," Walt said. "This is Babcock. He's trying out for goalie. He's slow and quick and stupid and smart and, I suppose, short and tall."

"No, sir," Babcock said. "Regular size. I'm fat, though."

"Fat *and* skinny, I suppose," Walt said.

"No, sir. Just fat." Babcock smiled.

"I'm not arguing," the coach said. "Jack. Would you show Babcock where the goal is, and what he's supposed to do?"

Jack took Babcock to the goal. Walt was mumbling to himself, "Slow but quick. Gimme a break."

We lined up to practice penalty shots. Babcock

stood in the goal. Jack stood behind the net. "Shoot," he said.

Dylan shot. The ball rolled straight to Babcock, who bent over and picked it up. "Is that it?" Babcock asked.

"Throw it back," Jack said.

Danny took a shot. His kick rolled toward the corner of the goal. Babcock leaped to his left and blocked it.

"Hey," Jack said.

Then it was my turn. I sent a perfect shot in the air toward the corner. Babcock jumped like a flying cannonball, stretched out both arms, and caught the ball in his fingertips.

"Outstanding!" Jack said.

Walt turned his face to the sky. "Thank you, great galloping banana slugs," he said to the clouds.

2.
Damaged Goods

After practice I walked home. I passed a couple of garbage cans that had been knocked over by dogs. Paper cups and Styrofoam meat trays were blowing along the street. There's a pack of wild dogs in town. People from over the hill bring their unwanted dogs here and abandon them. Some of them die. Some get adopted. And some learn to raid garbage cans and go wild.

My mother was making pizza. My sister Clover was practicing cartwheels on the rug. My little brother Dale was racing Matchbox cars down the stair rail.

My mom said, "Tom's late." Tom is my father. "He hasn't called. We'll just go ahead and eat without him. Hurry up and change your clothes, Boone."

I went to my room. As I took off my shorts, I

noticed out the window a foot, attached to a leg, on the back porch. I stepped into the hallway and looked out the window of the door to get a better angle of view and saw two feet in jogging shoes, one untied, and two legs in blue jeans. I assumed that they were attached to a body and that the body was sitting against the door down below the window where I couldn't see it.

So I opened the door.

A man's body fell at my feet. Now his head was in the hall, his legs still on the porch.

Was he dead?

No. Breathing.

He was asleep. He smelled like a broken bottle of whiskey. His name, I knew, was Damon Goodey, though most people called him Damaged Goods, or Goods for short. All the kids knew him. Grown-ups pointed him out as an example of how we might turn out if we messed up our lives. And now he lay at my feet. His mouth hung open; his nose needed wiping; his breathing was slow and raspy-sounding.

I ran back to the kitchen. My father had just arrived home and was hugging my mother. They hug for about a minute, and you can't interrupt them. What was odd about this hug was that he was only holding her with one hand, while the other was carrying a red five-gallon can. When they finished, my mother said, "Why aren't you in your clothes, Boone? Dinner's ready."

"Goods," I said. "Damon Goodey's here."

My father frowned. He set down the can. "What does he want?"

"He's asleep."

"Where?"

"In the hall."

"The hall?"

My mother said, "Do something, Tom. Dinner's ready."

I followed my father. I was still in my underpants. Dale and Clover followed me.

Goods hadn't moved.

"That *does* it," my father said. "Give me a hand."

My brother, my sister, my dad, and I all picked Damon Goodey up by the shoulders and pushed him back onto the porch. He was soft and heavy, kind of like moving a mattress. My dad slammed the door and locked it. Goods never opened his eyes.

"Wash your hands. All of you," my father said. "I've *had* it with this town. Dinner's ready. I'm calling the sheriff."

I asked, "What will they do?"

"Arrest him, I hope. Move him, at least."

"Won't he be mad?"

"I should think so."

"Couldn't he just stay on the porch until he wakes up?"

"No."

"We could carry him out to the side of the road."

"I'm not *touching* him again."

"Don't you want to help him?"

"No."

"You want him to go to jail?"

"Yes."

My dad went to the bathroom and washed his hands. Then he dialed 911.

"*Dad. Don't.* He'll *blame* us. He'll be *mad* at us."

"Fine. I'm mad at him." And he started speaking into the phone.

I ran down the hall and through the kitchen and out the front door and around the outside of the house to the back porch. I didn't think it was fair of my dad to call the sheriff without even trying to help him. Damon, I saw, had rolled over on his side. I grabbed his shoulder with both hands and shook it. His head rolled back and forth. His eyes opened for just a moment, then closed.

I shook him again.

His eyes opened for two seconds. Then shut. Then opened again for five seconds. Blinking. Then shut. His lips moved. "Water," he mumbled.

I got the hose. "Hold this," I said, and put it in his hands. "I'll go turn it on."

He held it. I turned on the hose faucet. Unfortunately, I turned it on a little too fast, and water shot out the end of the hose into Damon's face.

At least it woke him up.

He was sputtering and dripping. And furious.

"You have to go," I said. "The sheriff's coming."

"You called the sheriff on me?"

"No. *I* didn't. I'm telling you so you can — "

"I'll *get* you for this."

He tried to stand up but didn't quite make it. His legs buckled.

I backed away.

"You tried to *drown* me," he said. "You leave me alone. You ever call the sheriff again, and I'll *get* you. I *will*."

He stood up. The porch was wet where he'd lain. His clothes were soggy from the hose.

"I didn't do it," I said. "I'm trying to *help* you."

"I'll *get* you," he said.

Heading for the street, Damon Goodey shuffled slowly, shirt untucked, face unshaved, hair un-combed, shoe untied. He was, as my father had often said, one sorry mess of a man. And now, he was my enemy. All for trying to help him.

I put on my pants and went to dinner.

My father was mad. "You shouldn't have wakened him," he said, passing me the pizza.

I was mad, too. "You always say we should help people," I said, taking two slices.

"Did he appreciate it?" my dad asked.

"No. Now he hates me."

"There. See?"

"Now Tom," my mother said, "you don't help peo-ple just because they'll *appreciate* it."

"That's true," my father said. "But do you think you really helped him?"

"Yes," I said. "Now he won't go to jail."

"But by not sending him to jail, aren't we telling him that it's all right to be a drunk?"

"I never said that."

"Aren't we saying that it's all right for drunk drivers to slaughter people on the highway?"

"I never said *that*, either."

"No. You didn't. But I'm saying that the first step to curing a problem is to make the person face up to the fact that he *has* a problem. Sometimes, sending a person to jail is a way to make a person realize he's not just a drinker, he's a *drunk*." My father chewed thoughtfully for a moment. "Of course, in Damon's case, I don't think it would work."

"Why not? You just said — "

"Some people are beyond help. Some people are just plain *bad*."

My mother said, "Alcoholism *is* a disease, Tom."

"Yes," my father said. "But he's not just an alcoholic."

"Those are just rumors," my mom said.

"What rumors?" I said.

"Things you go to jail for," my dad said. "But never mind."

Clover said, "Why do they call him Goods?"

"Never mind," my father said.

"It's short for Damaged Goods," I said.

"What goods?" Clover asked.

"Never mind," my father said.

Clover said, "Once he told me, down at the lake, he said, 'Hey, little girl, I've got the goods.'"

My dad slammed his hand down on the table. The pizza jumped. "That *does* it," he shouted.

"What goods?" Clover asked again.

"Don't ever go *near* that man," my father shouted.

Clover looked frightened. "I won't," she said. And then, stubbornly, "What goods?"

"He wants . . . He's got . . ." My father waved his arms. He seemed to want to say two things at the same time, one with each arm. Finally he brought his left arm down. Gesturing with the right, he focused on one answer. "*Stolen* goods," he said. "I *knew* it. It isn't just a *rumor*. He steals things, then he sells them at that *bar*. I'd like to see him in *jail*. I'd like to see that Puerco Pub shut *down*. Damon Goodey is *scum*. Now he's bringing his *sleaze* to my *daughter*."

My mother said, "Calm down, Tom."

Sometimes my father gets to ranting and raving. I could see that this was going to be one of those times. He was waving his arms again, this time above his head. Then he brought his fists down and pounded them on the tabletop — the plates rattled — as he said, "I hope a giant meteorite falls out of the sky and lands right on that bar — that Puerco Pub. And *crushes* it. And *burns* it to dust."

"Tom!" my mother shouted.

My mother almost never shouts. We all fell silent. My father looked a little sheepish.

After a few moments, I said, "Walt goes to the Pub."

My dad said sarcastically, "Well, I hope he won't be

there when the meteorite hits. We wouldn't want to hurt the soccer coach."

I said, "Emma goes there." Emma is Danny's stepmother, sort of.

"All right, all right," my father said. "Lots of people go there. Mostly good decent people. And a few jerks. And their wild dogs."

My mom said, "You aren't mad at the Pub, Tom. You're mad at Damon Goodey."

My dad said, "Damon Goodey *is* the Pub. He's *always* there."

My mother said, "Every town has a bar, Tom."

"Not like this town," my father said, spreading his hands toward the view from the dining room window. You can see down the road where a man is living in a converted school bus with chickens scratching in his yard.

"You love this town," my mother said. "You know you do. That's why we live here. That's why you put up with that long drive to work. We've got the country, the mountains, clean air, wonderful redwood trees. . . ."

"And no gas station," my dad said.

I said, "Did you run out of gas again?"

"Yes. But this time I bought a five-gallon can and filled it with gas. I'm going to keep it in the garage. That way, next time I'm low on gas I can fill up before I leave, since I always seem to forget when I'm over the hill." He looked around the table. "So why is everybody giggling?"

"There's one other thing you seem to forget, Dad," I said. "You bought one of those cans last time you ran out of gas. Now you have two."

"Really? I don't remember that."

"That's another reason why you love this town," my mom said. "No gas stations. No McDonald's. No shopping mall."

"Yes," my dad said. "I love it. And that's why I hate that bar." He was calm now. "What a town. What a ramshackle sorry mess of a town. Which I happen to love."

San Puerco does look run down. Most of the houses look ready to collapse if you slammed the door too hard. Except ours and a few other new ones.

"And the people!" my father continued. "A whole town full of cranks and dreamers. Who I also happen to love. A bunch of *misfits*. They'd get run out of the suburbs even if they could afford to live there. Which they can't. The soccer coach drives a *Harley*. Where did we *get* these people? Out of a population of five hundred — and that includes children, ducks, and wild dogs — out of that tiny population we have five nuclear physicists. And twelve poets. *Twelve*."

One of those poets is my mom. And one of those nuclear physicists is Walt, my soccer coach. He works over the hill at a place where they smash atoms to see what's inside. Most people in town work over the hill — over the mountain, really — in the Silicon Valley, where the air is smoggy, the roads are ugly, and you can't even see any stars at night. My dad works over there. He's a computer engineer. He moved here when he married Mom. They couldn't afford the houses over the hill. Now, I don't think they'd live there even if they had the money. Like my mom said, Dad does love it here. Sometimes I hear him get up at three o'clock in the morning and go for a walk. He says he's going to check if the stars are still there. He has a friend across town who has an observatory in his backyard. They sit out there, look at the sky, and mostly I think they just talk.

My father says he doesn't need a whole lot of sleep. Sometimes he stays up half the night doing work on his computer.

One thing about my father: He's absentminded. Like with the gas. Which makes me think, sometimes, that he *does* need more sleep.

My mother was laughing to herself. She said, "Tom, if this is a town for cranks and dreamers, you qualify on both counts." Then she patted his hand.

Dale, my little brother, couldn't fall asleep. His room is next to mine. I could hear him rolling around on his bed, kicking his feet against the wall. I was sitting up in my own bed, mapping out a dungeon. Whenever he kicked the wall, it shook against my back.

The shaking was giving me a headache. Finally I went to Dale's room. At the same time, my mom decided to go in there.

"I can't *sleep*," Dale said.

"Keep trying," my mother said.

"How?" Dale asked.

"Just lie quietly. Sleep will come."

"But *how*?"

I wondered: How? How do you explain sleep? Here's a problem even grown-ups can't answer. You can explain how to kick a soccer ball: You move your foot this way, and the ball goes that way. But you don't move anything to fall asleep.

"Try counting," my mom said.

"I did," Dale said.

"Try thinking about something nice that you're going to do tomorrow."

"I did. I thought about taping pennies to a paper airplane to make it go faster. Now I want to get up and try it."

"Stay there," my mother said.

"Close your eyes," Clover said. She'd been standing at the door, listening.

"Why?" Dale asked.

"So you can sleep," Clover said. "You have to close your eyes to go to sleep."

"Nuh-uh," Dale said. "I sleep with my eyes open."

"No you don't," Clover said. "I've seen you. They're closed. Always. Everybody sleeps with their eyes closed."

"Really?"

"Uh-huh."

"Do you sleep with your eyes closed, Clover?"

"Yes."

"Do you, Mommy?"

"Yes, dear."

"Do you, Boone?"

"Yes. Always."

"Hmm." Dale closed his eyes. "I'll try it."

Back on my own bed, I heard no more kicking of the wall. I turned out the light, but now *I* couldn't sleep. I was thinking of all the billions of things you have to learn in this world and how sometimes, somebody forgets to tell you one. Nobody ever told Dale that people sleep with their eyes closed, not in the three years he's been on the planet. And by this time nobody would think to tell him because we expected him to already *know* it. He might have gone through the rest of his *life* not knowing to close his eyes.

Maybe there's something that somebody forgot to tell Damon Goodey, some simple thing like closing your eyes to go to sleep — like, maybe, that alcohol is *poison* — and that's why he's the way he is.

It's scary. What if there's something they forgot to tell *me*? Already today I've learned that a person can be slow but quick, and that a person may not always appreciate being helped, and probably some other things that I can't even think of right now. Every day I learn new stuff. What if I *miss* something?

Maybe that's why my father doesn't sleep much. He goes over to the observatory to learn all the stuff he slept through when he was a kid.

I closed my eyes.

I wondered, if I go to sleep now, what will I miss?

The passing of the stars and planets. The rising of the moon. The rush of the wind over the trees, the coming of the fog. Maybe, some night, the crash of a meteorite.

I don't know whether I'd been sleeping or not, but the next thing I knew I could sense the presence of somebody standing by my bed. I opened my eyes, and it was my father.

"I'm proud of you, Boone," he said.

"For what?"

"For wanting to help people. Even a worthless scum like Damon Goodey. You have good instincts. I'm sorry I yelled at you."

"You didn't yell at me. You were yelling at the Pub."

"I shouldn't yell. I should do something about that place."

"What can you do?"

"I don't know. But I'll think of something."

Then he kissed me good-night.

3.
Soliciting a Pledge

The next morning at school when I walked into the classroom, Mrs. Rule was stalking something with a flyswatter. She slapped. She missed. It was something big. It darted from the top of her desk to the ceiling to a shut window where it banged against the glass. Mrs. Rule followed. I sat down.

It was a bright orange dragonfly.

It came to rest on an unoccupied desk. Babcock was just walking into the room. Mrs. Rule crept up to the desk and raised the swatter. Babcock spotted the dragonfly, and a look of horror came over his face. He leaped across a desk. He crashed into the dragonfly's desk and fell to the floor. The dragonfly zipped across the room, found an open window, and disappeared into the sunshine. Mrs. Rule put her hands on her hips and stamped her foot.

"Mr. Babcock!" she said. "What is the meaning of this?"

Babcock was lying on the floor, clutching his side where it had struck the desk. "Sorry," he said. "I slipped."

At soccer practice, Walt ran us through some drills, then called us together for a meeting. "Your first game of the season is this coming Saturday." He stroked his beard as he spoke. "Babcock, you'll be goalie. Dylan, you're a fullback. And no daydreaming when the ball is coming toward you. Boone, halfback. You're our setup man, Boone. You're a good passer and great at positioning the ball, but you lack that killer instinct. Unlike Danny. Danny, center forward. Boone will set you up. You punch it in. Geraldine, you, too — you're a killer. Be up there with Danny."

Geraldine is the only girl on our team. We call her Hairball. That's what she looks like. A head of curly, tough, black hair about the size and shape of a basketball. She stands on the grass during a game, twisting a finger through a lock of hair as if soccer is the last thing on her mind — sometimes you can even hear her humming a song — and then suddenly the ball comes her way and she blasts it.

"One more thing," Walt said. "I just got a letter from my cousin in Australia. He's got a soccer team over there. He challenged us to a match. In Australia. Anybody interested?"

"Yeah!" we all shouted.

"I thought so," Walt said. "Anybody ever been to Australia before?"

"No," we all said.

"Well, let me tell you. Those kids over there are born with cleats on their feet. They sleep with soccer balls in their cribs. They suckle their babies on Gatorade. They don't learn to walk, they learn to dribble. Get the picture? They're *good*. If you guys want to look decent against them, we'll really have to work."

Danny said, "How do we get there?"

"We fly," Walt said.

"Who buys the tickets?" Danny said.

"We do."

Danny kicked the dirt. "Dsh," he said. Danny's father doesn't work much. He gets food stamps. They don't even have a phone. Or a car.

"We have to raise money," Walt said. "I know your father can't afford the tickets, Danny. It may be too much for some of the other kids, too. We'll have to raise a whole lot of money. Like, thousands of dollars."

Dylan said, "We could have a bake sale."

Danny groaned. "Dsh, Dylan. Can we make *thousands* of dollars on a bake sale?"

"We could if we baked marijuana brownies," Dylan said.

"Dylan!" Walt screamed.

"Hey, yeah!" Danny said. "We could — "

"Forget it!" Walt shouted. "And I'll try to forget I

ever *heard* that idea. Dylan, I want to have a talk with you when we get home. Great galloping banana slugs. Any other ideas?"

Hairball, with one finger twisting a lock of hair, said, "We could have a kickathon. Get people to sponsor us. Pledge money, so much per foot."

"That's *lame*," Danny said. "Who's going to get excited about paying to see how far we can kick a ball?"

"Got a better idea?" said Walt.

"I might," Babcock said. "What we need to do is perform a service. Something that needs to be done. If we want to get sponsors to pledge money, I mean people besides our own parents, we have to offer something useful."

"Like what?" Walt asked.

"What I've noticed," Babcock said, wiping his forehead, "is that nobody cleans up around here. The garbage trucks come and they empty the garbage cans, but nobody cleans the streets. The ditches are full of trash. We could clean it up. We could ask people to pledge, say, ten cents a pound. We could get a scale and weigh the trash each person brings in, and that's how much their sponsors would pay for. So, for example, if I collected fifty pounds of garbage, and somebody had pledged me ten cents a pound, he'd owe me five dollars. If I got ten people to pledge ten cents a pound, they'd owe me a total of fifty dollars."

"That sounds like a lot of *work*," Dylan said.

"Work," Babcock said, "is how you make money."

"Babcock," Walt said, smiling, "you're a born cap-
italist. I think you've got a good idea. Nobody can say
no to a kid who wants to clean up the garbage.
There're two hundred and fifty houses in this town.
There're eleven of you. I want each of you to get
twenty pledges. That means knocking on doors. I'll
get a scale. We'll make signs. Hey. I know. We'll call
it *The Trashathon*."

I told my dad we were going to Australia and I
wanted him to pledge twenty cents a pound to our
Trashathon.

"Australia? Trashathon?" he said. "My congratu-
lations to your coach. Those are *great* ideas for that
old hippie to come up with."

"Don't call him names," I said. "And it was Babcock
who thought of the Trashathon."

"Hippie is not an insult," my father said. "A hippie
was a person who believed in peace and love. What's
wrong with peace and love?"

"Hippies were crazy," I said. "They took drugs."

"So do doctors," my father said. "So do basketball
players. Anybody can be stupid. I'll pledge ten cents
a pound."

"Aw, Dad," I said. I felt strangely dizzy. "Make it
twenty."

"Ten's firm," he said. "If you want more money,
collect more trash."

Instead of answering him — or maybe it was a kind
of answer — I suddenly turned around and puked into

a wastebasket. I felt as if somebody had kicked me in the stomach.

I spent the next day in bed with the flu.

Friday I returned to school only to find out that all the other kids on the team had their twenty pledges. They'd knocked on every door in town except for Miser Tate's. A few people had turned them down (including Danny's own father, which wasn't a surprise); a few people were out of town; but most had pledged something in the neighborhood of ten cents a pound. The lowest pledge was a nickle; the highest, a quarter.

Which left me with nobody to get a pledge from. I could work my butt off and collect a hundred pounds of trash, and all I'd have to show for it would be my father's cheapo pledge of ten cents a pound.

"Well," Danny said with a snicker, "you could always try Miser Tate."

I groaned.

Babcock said, "Who's Miser Tate?"

"His name is Meyer Tate," I said. "I went to his house once on Halloween. He gave me a cup of *water*."

"Does he have money?" Babcock asked.

"Sure," I said. "He owns a bunch of houses. All the houses on his street. Like Danny's."

"Yep," Danny said. "He's our landlord." Danny's house leans to one side and would fall over except that it's propped against the trunk of a redwood tree. He says that every morning he has to dust the termite wings off his kitchen table before he eats his cereal.

There're a couple of old junker cars in his yard which were there when he and his father moved in and which Tate refuses to have hauled away. The faucets drip. The toilet rocks back and forth when you sit on it. Tate's other houses are the same way, except for the one he lives in himself.

"So what's to lose?" Babcock said. "You could try him."

"There're signs on his gate," I said. "NO TRESPASSING. KEEP OUT. NO SOLICITORS. NO MISSIONARIES. BEWARE OF DOG. Except, he doesn't even have a dog."

"So you're scared?" Babcock asked.

"I went there on Halloween," I said. "I ought to be able to do it in broad daylight." I didn't mention that I'd only done it on Halloween on a dare. And it was spooky walking up his driveway. Tate didn't waste his money on outdoor lighting. "Still," I said, "I think it's a waste of time."

"I'll come with you," Babcock said. "If you want."

I wanted.

Babcock and I walked across town to Meyer Tate's. On the way we had to pass the lake in the center of town. It's just a small pond surrounded by blackberries, poison oak, and some scruffy cottonwoods. About a dozen ducks live there, and one mean old goose who sometimes comes out in the road and attacks dogs or people or even cars. Once my dad made the mistake of honking his car horn at the goose, and the goose started honking back and pecking at the

bumper. Our old Volkswagen bus had spoken his lan-
guage, and whatever it said, he didn't like it. It took
ten minutes to get by him.

At the corner of the pond next to the road, the
teenagers like to gather with their trucks. They brag,
play loud music, drink beer when they can get it, and
haul logs. They try to see who can chain the heaviest
old redwood log to the back of his truck, spin his
wheels, make a huge cloud of dust, and drag it.

As we walked toward them now, the biggest pickup
of all was growling and bucking, trying to budge a
gigantic old hulk of a log.

Babcock stopped and watched for a moment. He
shook his head. "Who buys big trucks, I wonder?" he
asked.

"Short people," I said. I'd asked that same question
to my father, and that's what he said. And it's true.
The biggest man in town, Elmer Thompson, a logger,
drives a little Honda Civic. When he gets out of that
tiny car, it looks like one of those clown acts at the
circus — you wonder how he ever fit in there. But
the smallest driver in town, who happens to be Jack
Bean, our assistant soccer coach, has the biggest
truck, the one we were watching — a one-ton Dodge
with tires the size of tractors and a motor that could
drive a freight train. He calls it The Beanstalk because
it's up so high he needs a ladder to climb into the
cab. As we watched, he managed to shake the log over
about an inch.

"Hurray!" I shouted.

Jack saw us. He waved.

I waved back.

Babcock wasn't looking. His head was turned toward the lake. His eyes were following something. I saw his lips move just a fraction as if he was saying something, but I could hear no sound. Then Babcock held out his hand. Again his lips moved, and again I heard no sound.

A glorious green dragonfly alighted on his outstretched hand.

Now Babcock was moving his lips constantly. Slowly he pulled his hand close to his body until the dragonfly was just in front of his face. The wings quivered, sparkling in the sunlight. The body flashed with green fire.

Babcock stretched his hand out again away from his body. His lips stopped their silent movement.

The dragonfly rustled its wings, and was gone like a bullet.

"Wow!" I said. "How do you do that?"

"I talk to them," he said.

"I couldn't hear anything," I said.

"They can," he said.

We walked on. We passed Danny's house and climbed the hill toward Meyer Tate's. A couple of dogs started following us.

There was something I wanted to ask Babcock. I said, "Is your father a nuclear physicist?" It wasn't such a weird question when you remember that we already have five nuclear physicists in town, and also when you consider Babcock's interest in science, or at least in rocks and dragonflies.

"No," Babcock said. "He runs a car repair shop in Pulgas Park."

"For Volvos?"

"For anything."

My dad's name for Pulgas Park is Volvoville because that's what everybody seems to drive over there.

I said, "Was it your dad who named you Babcock?"

Babcock stopped walking. I think he needed a rest anyway. The hill was a hard climb. The dogs, seeing that we'd stopped, started sniffing out some black-berry bushes.

Babcock looked me in the eye. He said, "My dad didn't name me Babcock. I *am* Babcock."

"So," I said, "what's *his* name?"

Babcock didn't say anything for a few moments. Then he shrugged. "All right," he said. He smiled. It wasn't an entirely friendly smile. "You want to know about my name."

"I guess that's what I was poking around about," I said.

"I *guess*," Babcock said with an exasperated sigh. "All right. My father's name is Thomas Babcock. So he didn't have to name me Babcock. I get that name *automatically*."

"Didn't he give you any other name? Is it horrible? Percy? Egbert? Arvid?"

"No no. He didn't give me any other name. My mom and dad left it blank. They wanted me to choose my own name when I was old enough to talk."

"Can they *do* that?"

"Sure. You can name a kid — or not name him — anything you want."

"So what did you choose?"

"At first I thought about Donald. After Donald Duck. Only I pronounced it Dongle. I mean that's how little I was. But my parents kind of discouraged me from naming myself after a cartoon. So then I wanted to be Big Bird. Big Bird Babcock. But they kind of discouraged that one, too. Then I saw *The Wizard of Oz* and decided to name myself Dorothy. You can imagine what they thought of *that* idea. By this time I think they were sorry they ever gave me a choice, so they started suggesting names. Like, Bret. Bret Babcock. They liked that. I hated it. I hated every name they came up with. So finally, I came up with a name of my own. I told them I wanted to be Two One Five Five Two."

Babcock smiled to himself.

"So is that your name?" I asked. "Two One Five Five Two?"

"No," Babcock said. "The people at the county office wouldn't let us change the birth certificate. It's too late. I can never have another name."

"But we could *call* you that. Do you want to be called Two One Five Five Two?"

"No." He shook his head. His cheeks jiggled. "Not anymore. I'm quite happy to be who I am Babcock. Just plain Babcock." He started walking again. The dogs followed. "But when I get older," Babcock said, "I'm gonna have a rock-and-roll band. And we're gonna name it Two One Five Five Two."

We came to Meyer Tate's gate with all its signs. It was locked.

"You sure he doesn't have a dog?" Babcock asked.

"Don't worry," I said. "He *hates* dogs."

We climbed over the gate leaving the dogs behind, walked up the driveway past his shiny white Mercedes, and knocked on the door. There was no doorbell. No doorknocker. He wasn't going to encourage visitation.

The door opened.

"What do you want?"

Meyer Tate had white hair. Thin lips. He was dressed in a bathrobe — at four o'clock in the afternoon.

Suddenly I realized that I hadn't given a single thought to planning what I was going to say. I searched for words. My mind went almost blank.

"It's . . . us," I said.

"Oh, really?" he said.

"We — uh — came."

"Yes?"

"We're having. A. A Trashathon," I said.

"A what?"

"A pledge," I said. "You put it on a scale, and then we tell you the garbage."

"What?"

"A scale. We weigh the pledge. For money. I mean,

we tell you the trash. We need the garbage for Australia. It's soccer, you know."

Tate looked over at Babcock, who was laughing so hard he had to hold his sides or else I think they might have shaken loose.

Tate said, "Are you boys playing some sort of a joke on me?"

"No," I said.

"We want to pick up garbage," Babcock said. "Clean up the town. It's for our soccer team. We're trying to raise money. We're asking everybody in town to pledge so much per pound to one of us. In this case, Boone here wants a pledge. Then, however much garbage he collects, you pay for."

"Did you see the sign on my gate?" Meyer Tate said.

"Yes," Babcock said.

"It says NO SOLICITORS."

"Yes, sir," Babcock said.

"But I'll make an exception," Meyer Tate said. "I approve of boys cleaning up the town. I'll make a pledge."

"Thank you," I said. "How much can I put you down for?"

"One cent."

"OK," I said. "Thank you."

You were supposed to get people to sign pledge cards, but for one penny I wasn't going to bother. I turned to go. I saw Babcock standing there. He wasn't moving, but his face was getting sweatier and sweatier. Then he exploded. "That's an *insult*. One cent! He could collect a whole *ton* of trash, and you'd only owe a few bucks! Why *bother*? You're supposed to *motivate* him. He's providing a *service*. You're supposed to make it worth his while to *do* all this work. How much do you think he can get? A hundred pounds? It could take him *all day* to find a hundred pounds of trash. And you'd only owe him *one* dollar! You expect him to work all day for one dollar?"

I looked at Meyer Tate. I expected to see him slamming the door. Instead, he was standing with his hands on his hips, staring at Babcock. His bathrobe was slipping open. His chest was hairy and gray.

"Young man," he said, "what is your name?"

"Babcock, sir."

"Babcock. Hmm," Tate said, filing the name away in his mind.

"Let's go," I said.

"Wait," Tate said. "I like your spunk, Babcock. I think you understand business. Motivation. Free enterprise. Unlike most of the people in this town. They don't like me. And do you know why they don't like me? It's because I know how to make a *profit*. I know how to make a *deal*. I know how to use a deal to my own *advantage*."

"They might like you better," Babcock said, "if you made a decent pledge to help clean up the town."

"I will," Tate said. "By golly, I will. I tell you what. I'll pledge one dollar a pound. Go ahead. Get a hundred pounds. Don't worry, I can add. But I make one condition. You have to collect it on this street. After all, I own it. I might as well get my own street cleaned up for the money. I only hope your friend is better at picking up trash than he is at explaining the meaning of Trashathon."

"It's a deal," I said. "Sign here."

"Just a minute," Babcock said. "Do you mean one dollar *plus* the one penny you already pledged? For a total of one dollar and one cent?"

Tate pulled his bathrobe closed. He gave Babcock a look that reminded me of Mrs. Rule. He shook his head. I think he was already regretting that he'd made the pledge. But then he smiled. His lips were crooked as if he wasn't used to doing it very often.

"All right," he said.

And he signed the pledge for one dollar and one cent per pound.

Walking back down the hill from Meyer Tate's house, we checked out the garbage in the ditches. So did the dogs. Mostly it was soda cans and candy wrappers, but down at the bottom across from Danny's house there was a double mattress that probably weighed thirty pounds. And if it rained between now and the Trashathon, it would weigh even more.

"Maybe we could get Danny to soak it with a hose," Babcock said.

My father was late for dinner. We waited a half hour, then went ahead and ate without him. At last, at eight o'clock, he arrived.

"Ran out of gas," he said, and he hugged my mom.

"Did you buy a five-gallon can to keep in the garage?" I asked.

He didn't answer for a minute until he let go of the hug. Then he said, "Of course not. I've already got two."

That night I awoke in darkness. I could hear my dad clumping around in the closet. I looked at my clock: 2:32. I got up.

The light from the closet nearly blinded me. My father was pulling on his Nikes.

"Going to the observatory?" I said.

"Yep."

"Can I come?"

He looked up from the knot he was tying.

"Not tonight," he said. "You need your sleep. School tomorrow."

"So do you," I said. "You have to *work* tomorrow. You'll run out of *gas* again."

"No, I won't," he said. "I just filled it up today."

"Were you listening to a tape when you ran out of gas?"

"Yes."

"Were you singing?"

"Probably. I don't remember."

He has about two dozen tapes of old rock and roll. He calls it do-wop. He sings along with them in *falsetto*. I'm sure that's why he runs out of gas — he's too busy singing to look at the gas gauge. I just hope none of my friends ever hear him.

"Meyer Tate pledged one dollar and one cent to the Trashathon," I said.

"Really? That's amazing."

"But I have to collect it on his street."

"That seems fair."

"You want to raise your pledge?"

"No."

"This weekend can I go to the observatory?"

"I'll ask Patrick."

"You won't forget?"

"Of course not." He finished tying his Nikes. "Wait a minute," he said. "So now you're going to collect all your trash on Meyer Tate's street?"

"Right."

"So I'm paying ten cents a pound to help Tate clean *his* street?"

I hadn't thought of that. I had to laugh. "Thanks, Dad," I said. "And I'm sure Meyer Tate thanks you, too."

It was just as Tate had said. He certainly did know how to make a deal.

4.
The Game

Saturday morning we had our first soccer game of the year. We play all our games over the hill in Pulgas Park. They're willing to let us into their league, especially since they always beat us, but they aren't willing to drive to our town. My dad says they're afraid we'll steal the hubcaps off their Volvos, but I think he's kidding.

Danny and I rode over with Jack Bean in the Beanstalk. Now *that's* the way to make an entrance to a soccer game. As we jumped down from that high cab, every kid on both teams practically drooled with envy. On our side of the field were parked the Beanstalk, Walt's Harley, a dented Ford Econovan, a rusty Toyota, and a Chevy pickup with lumber racks. On the other side were three shiny Volvo station wagons, a

42

Mercedes, a sleek Jaguar, and a new Buick Cutlass Supreme.

Jack went over to talk with Walt. Danny and I walked onto the field and started kicking the ball around. I shanked one. It landed in a pile of clothes on the other team's side of the field. Danny ran over with me to fetch the ball. It was lying on some sweatshirts and a pair of designer jeans with shiny silver stars around the pockets. I picked up the ball. Danny reached down and rearranged the pile a bit. Then we both ran back onto the field.

"What'd you do?" I asked.

"Tidying up," Danny said, and he went over to our side of the field and put something in the Beanstalk.

Jack beckoned me to him. "See that guy?" he said, pointing to a tall kid with long, black hair on the other side of the field. He wore their number One. "He's their point man. Stop him, and we stop their team. I want you to dog him, Boone. He's your man. Stay with him wherever he goes. Forget positions. Forget zones. You're his shadow. Take it from me: Big guys get frustrated by speedy little guys. Then they press too hard and make mistakes."

We played a tough game. Most of the action was down at our own end of the field where they always were threatening to score. Number One was tall and strong and could outrun me in a straight race, but in soccer it's not always an advantage to be big, and on some moves I could be quicker. As Babcock would say, I was slower but quicker. And I could see number One was getting annoyed having a little guy steal his ball away or block his kicks. Of course, sometimes he got around me, and then Babcock made a couple of nice saves.

Babcock had bought cleats and shinguards. He wore pants that were cut off just below the knee.

Walt was running along the sidelines yelling, "Dylan, wake up! Geraldine, watch the ball! Babcock, move up! Danny, mark your man! Boone, hurry up!" I've sometimes wondered if maybe the reason Walt looks so old is that he ages five years every time he coaches a soccer game.

In the third quarter, Dylan, playing fullback and paying attention for a change, got his toe on the ball and found Geraldine all alone in the center of the field. Geraldine let go of her hair and broke loose with the ball, raced downfield, dribbled right around a fullback, and punched the ball into the corner of the goal. Way to go, Hairball! We led, one to nothing.

The other team kicked off. Number One took the ball and headed straight at me. I made a move for the ball and suddenly felt myself flying through the air. I landed about four feet away. My eye was exploding with pain. Dimly, I heard a whistle blowing, and way far away it seemed Walt was screaming, "Foul!"

Number One had socked me with an elbow right below my eye.

Play stopped. Jack Bean was standing over me, asking how many fingers he was holding in front of my face. I couldn't answer. The fingers kept floating, and the number kept changing.

"Hey, Boone," Danny said. "Dsh. Come on. *Dsh!*"

"Okay," I said. I looked at the fingers again. "Three," I said, and I stood up.

Now our team had an indirect kick, but it didn't do us any good.

Play continued. A few minutes later, number One got the ball again. I covered him, didn't bite at his fake, and stole the ball from between his feet. I started running — and went tumbling head over heels.

Again, the whistle.

"Tripping!" the ref said, and he showed number One the Yellow Card.

Again we took an indirect kick, and again we couldn't take advantage of it.

My eye was throbbing with pain. Now, covering number One, I kept a few extra feet away from him so he couldn't elbow me or trip me. I guess that was what he wanted, because I couldn't cover him as closely that way. He took the ball straight downfield, passed around Dylan to another player, took a pass back, and — just like that — scored a goal.

It was my fault, for backing off.

I kicked off with a pass to Danny. Danny passed to Geraldine, who took the ball into the corner and lofted a pass near the goal. I jumped up to head the ball when suddenly a shoulder slammed into my side. I went flying backward and upside down. I landed on

my head at the feet of number One and then felt a
kick in my side. It hurt so much, I had to close my
eyes. The last thing I saw was Babcock running —
actually *running* — toward us from the other end of
the field. Through the pain with my eyes closed I
heard a shout, a *whump*, a cheer (from Danny), and
a whistle blowing.

I opened my eyes.

There sat Babcock on top of number One.

Walt was cheering and whistling.

The ref showed Babcock the Yellow Card, and number One, the Red Card. Number One was out of the
game, and we had a penalty kick.

Geraldine lined up. She faked right but kicked left.
The goalie was leaning to the right. She scored.

Two to one.

A minute later, the game was over. That is, the
refereed part of the game was over. I saw number
One stomping across the field carrying a sweatshirt
and the pair of designer jeans with the silver stars.
He marched right up to me.

"You!" he said. "Where's my pocketknife?"

"I don't know," I said.

He was ready to fight. He was six inches taller and
fifty pounds heavier, and I was already feeling beat
up from the game. I could scarcely see out of my hurt
eye. I had a big bump on the top of my head and a
tender bruise in my ribs.

Number One shoved me on the chest.

I staggered backward.

He put his face right up in front of mine and said, "I saw you over there before the game. You took my pocketknife."

"No I didn't."

"Liar!"

Walt came up from behind me and placed a hand on my shoulder. I was mighty glad to feel it there. Number One's coach stood behind number One, placed a hand on *his* shoulder, and said, "That's the last straw. We don't have to let you and your bandits into this league, you know. I knew there'd be stealing. Next year, I'm going to see to it that your team doesn't play."

Walt turned me by the shoulder and looked me in the eye — the one that I could see through. His white beard was just inches from my face. "Boone," he said, "did you take that boy's pocketknife?"

"No," I said.

"Word of honor?" Walt said.

"Word of honor," I said.

"Then I believe you," Walt said.

At that moment, those three words — I believe you — were the sweetest music I'd ever heard.

Walt turned to the other coach. "He says he didn't take it, and I say he didn't take it. I give you my word."

"Jimmy," the other coach said to number One, "are you sure you didn't drop it somewhere?"

Number One said, "I had it just before the game."

The coach said, "Go over there and look around on the ground. Maybe it fell out."

I walked to the Beanstalk. I had a pretty good idea where that knife was. Danny was already sitting in the cab.

"Danny," I said, "did you steal that knife?"

"Dsh," Danny said. "Sorry, Boone. Thanks for taking the heat."

"Danny, you can't do that," I said.

"You certainly can't," Jack Bean said. I hadn't known he'd been standing on the other side of the truck. "Come on, Danny. We're going to have a talk with Walt."

Walt made Danny walk across the field with him, give back the knife, and apologize. Afterward, I saw the other coach shaking Danny's hand, so I guess we'll get to play in the league next year.

Danny, Jack, and I climbed into the Beanstalk.

Walt swung a leg over his motorcycle and then called up to Danny, "Hey. Why'd you take it?"

Danny hung his head out the window. "They've got so much. And I've got so little. It isn't *fair*."

Walt ran a hand through his beard. "Life isn't fair," he said. He kicked down on the starter, and the Harley roared to life. He called out, "But you gotta play a good game anyway," and then he took off.

Riding home, I told Danny that if he ever put me in a position like that again, I *would* snitch on him. Stealing is stealing.

"All right," he said. "All right."

But I don't think I really got through to him. I think he was agreeing that stealing is risky to yourself and to your friendships, but not that stealing is *wrong*.

I feel sorry for Danny. It isn't fair what he got for a family. His mother died when he was a baby. About all he knows about her is that she was born in Mazatlán, and she was beautiful. He has a photo of her in a white dress, her wedding dress. His father was born in Oklahoma. He's still a Sooners fan. He spent two years in the VA Hospital — he was in Vietnam and it did something to his brain. Now he's home, if you can call that shack they live in a home, but he's still weird. He watches war movies and football games all day on television, and every night he goes to the Pub. Off and on, he works at a gravel quarry five miles out of town. He doesn't know if Danny's home or if he gets fed or even if he sleeps at night. Danny had to spend two years living in the Catholic Home, which is a place for orphans and kids who for some reason or other can't live with their parents. That's where he learned to fight. And steal, I suppose. After the Home, he said, living with his father was like going from the House of Horrors to Disneyland. He told me once, if they tried to send him back there, he'd run away. He'd rather have no home than that Home.

Danny's world is so different from mine, sometimes I think we live on two different planets in two different dimensions where we can see each other and talk to each other, but we can't cross over.

Now there's Emma. She moved in with Danny's father a few months ago. I guess that would make her Danny's stepmother, but Danny doesn't think so. She's shy. She wears long sleeves and gloves all the time. Danny says she has tattoos on her arms and the back of her hands and that the flesh is ghostly white, but I've never seen them. She has a scar across her forehead and down her nose. She wears her bangs long to cover her forehead. Danny says she won't go anywhere — not even the store — unless she absolutely has to. Except the Pub. She goes there every night. In one way, at least, she's improved Danny's life because she has her own car, an old Chevelle with a scrunched-up rear end and no bumpers. Once she drove Danny to a summer league soccer game and stayed in the car where she couldn't see a thing while all the other grown-ups were on the sidelines, cheering. Danny scored two goals that day. When my father tapped on her window and invited her to come out, she said, "I can't. I'm too ugly."

She *does* look weird, if you ask me. She's all bosom and no waist. But my dad says she's "Va-va-voom," whatever that means. And I've seen Walt looking at her in a funny way.

Like I say, Danny lives in another dimension. And like Walt says, life isn't fair. But you've got to play a good game, anyway. The trouble is, in soccer the rules are clear and the goal is obvious. In life, the rules seem to *change* all the time, and I don't know *what* the goal is, much less *where*. Maybe Walt knows. I

don't think Danny's father does. If life is a game of
soccer, Danny's father is on the bench.

Anyway, Danny stays on the street or comes over
to my house whenever he can, especially at mealtimes.
Sometimes he spends the night. My mom always tells
him to phone home and tell his dad where he is. He's
never told her that his house doesn't have a phone.
He dials Directory Assistance. Then he pretends to be
asking his dad if he can spend the night.

I asked him, "What does your dad say if you don't
come home at night?"

"Nothing," Danny said. "If he notices. Which he
don't. And I don't say nothing if *he* don't come home."

My mother used to teach English. I couldn't talk
like Danny even if I wanted to, which I don't. I like
learning new words, especially big ones.

Maybe I'll ask my mom what Va-va-voom means.

"Hey Danny," I said. "You want to spend the night
at my house?" That was my way of telling him that
I wasn't holding a grudge about the pocketknife.

"Dsh," he said, which was his way of saying,
Thanks.

5.
A Studebaker,
a Crossbow,
and a Can of Beer

When Jack Bean pulled the Beanstalk into town with Danny and me riding high inside, we saw my father standing at the side of the road with four curious dogs beside an old hulk of a car that must have been abandoned just last night, since I'd never seen it before. Jack parked right next to him, and we all jumped down from the cab.

"Hey Dad!" I said. "We won!"

He saw me, and he looked horrified. "Won what?" he said. "A war?"

"The *game*."

"You've got a black eye."

"I do?"

"A beaut."

"What are you doing?"

He pointed at the abandoned car. "Fifty-two Studebaker," he said.

It had a crushed fender. No fabric on the seats. And rust, rust, rust.

My father said, "When I was a kid, my family had a fifty-two Studebaker. Best car we ever had. I think I'm going to try to start this old boy up and move it to our house before the county tows it away."

People are always abandoning cars in San Puerco the same as they abandon dogs. The sheriff tags the cars with a red sticker, and three days later they bring in a tow truck. I don't know why the people don't just leave the old wrecks in their own town to be hauled away. Maybe they're afraid somebody will recognize them. Of course, the county will only tow cars that are on the side of the street. If they're parked on private property, like the two old junkers around Danny's house, the landowner has to pay for the tow. Which Miser Tate will never do. They don't have tires, or I bet he'd *push* them out onto the road. They've been there so long, they've got sapling trees growing out through the windows, rooted in the seats. When Danny's father moved in, Tate told him, "They're not my cars. They're yours. You can sell them if you want." Of course, they're worthless.

My dad started fiddling under the steering wheel. He pulled two wires loose. He sat down on what was left of the front seat, pushed down the clutch, and touched the two wires together.

The engine cranked, but it wouldn't catch.

He opened the hood. He put it in neutral and told me to put the two wires together while he tinkered with the motor.

"Now!" he'd say. Then, "Hold it!" Then, "Now!"

For a half hour until the battery wore down, he tried to get that motor started. Then he unscrewed the gas cap and poked a stick into the tank.

Dry.

"Later," he said. "At least I've found the problem. Let's go home and have some lunch. They haven't even tagged this guy yet. I've got plenty of time."

"Once you get it home, Dad, what are you going to do with it?"

"Play with it. Fix it up."

He looked like a kid who'd just been promised a new toy.

Danny had lunch at my house.

After lunch, we went out. We were talking about the Trasnathon, which would be tomorrow. We checked out some ditches just to see what kind of haul we could expect to make.

In one ditch, Danny found an old inner tube, a big one, large enough for the Beanstalk or a farm tractor.

"Dsh!" he said.

"Two pounds," I said.

"No," he said. "A slingshot. A *monster* slingshot."

Back at my house we found a forked branch that had fallen from a Douglas fir. The wood was as thick as my arm. We hauled it to the garage where my dad keeps some tools I can use. Danny sawed off the ends of the branch until it was a Y-shape, about four feet tall. With shears Danny cut the inner tube across the middle and tied each end to the forks of the branch. Then he held the slingshot with his left hand, placed a rock about the size of a potato into the rubber, and tried to pull it back with his right hand. The wood was so heavy it wobbled in his hand, and the inner tube was so strong he could scarcely budge it.

"You hold it," he said. "I'll pull."

I placed the bottom between my feet and held the crotch of the fork with both hands. Danny put both hands on the rubber. He pulled. I leaned back, way back, and crouched with my head down so I'd be out of the line of fire. Danny leaned back with his feet propped against mine. The inner tube started to stretch. . . .

Snap!

The branch broke. Danny flew backward and somersaulted onto the floor of the garage into a pile of sawdust and oil with his head banging into my father's five-gallon cans of gasoline.

"Shut up," he said.

He stood up, brushed himself off, and walked out to the yard. I followed.

"There," he said. He was pointing down at a big old redwood branch about as thick as my leg. It was so heavy, we couldn't even move it. We brought out my father's pruning saw. The wood was so wet, it squirted us as we cut it. Danny untied the inner tube from the broken branch and retied it to the redwood.

We had a gigantic slingshot about six feet tall — taller than we were, except it was lying on the ground. It was still too heavy to move, but working together we were able to lift the forked end up to a standing position. It wobbled. It must have weighed a hundred pounds. It was impossible to keep it steady. I held it upright, swaying like a tree in the wind, and I leaned backward while Danny pulled back on the tube with the potato-rock inside. The rubber barely moved. Danny clenched his teeth, shut his eyes, bulged the muscles in his arm — and I lost it. The weight of the thing, plus Danny's pulling, ripped the slingshot right out of my hands. Danny fell backwards, with the sling-shot on top of him.

He was pinned, same as when Babcock sat on him. His head was in the fork.

"Shut up," he said.

"I didn't say anything."

"Just shut up," he said.

He pushed and I pulled, and we got him free.

"We need a tree," he said.

We found one, an oak with its trunk split about five feet above the ground. We tied the inner tube to the two sides of the trunk. Now we were both free to pull back on the rubber. We braced our feet against the trunk.

We pulled.

It stretched.

"On three," Danny said. "One, two, *three*."

Thwang!

The rock whistled out and across the yard — and hit smack dab in the middle of a big old redwood tree.

I looked at Danny.

Danny looked at me.

We both had just realized that we couldn't rotate the tree, we couldn't *aim*, we could only shoot at the redwood tree until we bombed it to death, which didn't seem very exciting. Or we could reverse the direction, but then we'd hit my house.

Silently, grimly, Danny untied the inner tube and carried it to the garage. I followed with my hands in my pockets.

Danny doesn't quit.

With the shears he cut a strip of rubber out of the inner tube. From the yard he selected a flexible stick of wood. He made a bow. Trouble was, when he pulled on the rubber, the knots slipped down from the end of the stick. He tried tying them tighter. Then the trouble was, when he pulled on the rubber, the stick broke. So he went out and found a thicker stick. He tied the ends tight, pulled back on the bow, way, way back — and the rubber broke and slapped him in the face.

Danny heaved the broken bow out the open door of the garage.

"Let's make a gun," he said.

"A *gun*?" I said.

He showed me how. From a pile of wood scraps

Danny found some one-by-twos. He sawed them, then nailed them together in the shape of a pistol. At the rear end of the barrel he used my father's hot-melt glue gun to attach a clothespin, the kind with wire springs. He sawed a notch at the front end of the barrel.

He stretched a rubber band from the notch at the front of the barrel to the clothespin at the rear. He held the pistol by the handle, put his thumb on the clothespin, and pressed it open. The rubber band shot across the garage.

We went outside and shot at each other until we'd lost all my dad's rubber bands.

"Wow, Danny! That was great," I said. "We made slingshots, bows, and then guns. We made everything."

"Yeah."

"About the only thing we couldn't make was a crossbow."

Danny's eyes lit up.

He built it out of two-by-fours. It was shaped like a T. He tied the inner tube to the ends, then screwed it on with washers, then nailed a block of wood on top of it just to make sure it held. At the base of the T he drilled a hole with my father's power drill, which I didn't think we were even allowed to use, but Danny didn't ask. He cut a piece of dowel to slip into the hole.

It took the strength of both of us pulling as hard as we could with our hands on the inner tube and our feet pushing on the bars of the T to stretch the rubber back to where the dowel could hold it in place. Now it was cocked. The rubber was so tight, it quivered like a guitar string.

Danny took a pencil off my father's workbench and placed it in the crotch of the inner tube, just above the dowel. With one hand he held the pencil in place; with the other he pulled down on the dowel.

Shlp!

The pencil flew out the open doorway of the garage and disappeared through some bushes in the yard.

Danny grabbed another pencil. "Come on!" he said.

"Where?"

"I dunno. Just come on."

We walked down toward the lake.

"Help me load this thing," Danny said.

Together we stretched the inner tube back until it was held at the bottom by the dowel. Some ducks, and the mean old goose, started swimming over to see if we were going to throw any bread crumbs. Danny lifted the crossbow, pointed it out over the pond, and set the pencil into the crotch. He sighted down the barrel.

I saw where he was aiming — right at the goose! His finger went to the dowel.

I jumped. I grabbed for Danny just as he pulled out the dowel.

Shlp!

The pencil shot through the air and struck the trunk of a cottonwood tree.

"You made me miss!" Danny shouted.

I snatched the crossbow out of his hand.

"Hey! Gimme!" he shouted.

"No," I said. "You're not using my house, my wood, my tools, to build something to *kill* things with."

"They're not yours. They're your father's."

"He wouldn't allow it, either."

"Dsh," Danny said. It was like a spit. "Then you're as bad as he is."

"No," I said. "I'm as *good* as he is."

For a moment, Danny stared at me hard. Then he said, "What did you think we were building it for?"

"For fun."

"You don't build a weapon for *fun*." Danny kicked his foot in the dirt. Then he brightened up. "Let's see what happened to the pencil."

We found it. The pencil had embedded itself two inches deep in the soft wood of the tree.

"Wow!" Danny said. "Think what that would've done to the goose!"

"I'm thinking," I said. And I went straight home and put that crossbow under the workbench in the garage, and then I closed the garage door.

"Some friend you are," Danny said.

"Some friend *you* are," I said.

We stared at each other. Then we each broke into a grin.

"Hey, did I tell you about Miser Tate?" I said. "He pledged a dollar and one cent a pound for the Trashathon."

"You're kidding. Miser Tate?"

"Babcock shamed him into it. But he said I had to collect it all on his street. Your street. And there's a double mattress in the ditch right across from your house. I thought maybe you could soak it with a hose, so it'd weigh more."

"Yeah. Let's do it."

We walked over to Danny's house. I looked in the ditch across from his house — and the mattress was *gone*.

"Look at that," Danny said. He was pointing up the street.

Miser Tate was walking along the road, dragging a garbage can. He was picking up all the trash he could find. On the hill below him, he'd picked the ground clean as a whistle.

Danny said, "What's a dollar and a cent times nothing?"

"Nothing," I said.

"Good math," Danny said. "A-plus."

"You know what Tate said to me when he made that pledge? He said, 'Don't worry. I can add.' "

Danny and I watched as he picked up an old newspaper and dumped it in the garbage can.

"Looks like he can also subtract," Danny said.

Walking back home, Danny and I were passing the abandoned Studebaker when we saw that the door was open. On the front seat a body was slouched under the steering wheel. There sat Damon Goodey with a sullen stare and a six-pack of beer.

"Damaged Goods," Danny muttered.

"If life was a soccer game," I said, "Damon Goodey would have a Yellow Card."

"His life is a baseball game," Danny said. "And he's the losing pitcher."

I knew what he meant. Damon Goodey had been a minor league pitcher for seven years, mostly in Fresno. He was fast but wild. Too wild, they say. Both on and off the field.

Goodey glared at me as we walked by, but he didn't say anything.

Damon Goodey didn't have a house or even a room to live in. He'd been living in a trailer outside of town until last spring, when the owner kicked him out. Everybody had hoped he'd leave San Puerco after that, but instead he hung around at the Pub and slept under trees or in abandoned cars or, once, of course, on my back porch.

My father would be angry when he learned that Damon Goodey had moved into the Studebaker that he'd wanted to fix up.

Then, as we were walking away, suddenly I felt a *thump* and pain as if somebody had thrown a rock into my back, and I fell forward onto my hands and knees, scraping the skin on my hands.

A full can of beer rolled away and across the street.

Damon Goodey was laughing. He'd stepped out of the Studebaker to make the throw.

Danny shouted something at Goods, something I

guess I shouldn't repeat. Goods shouted back: "Shut up, you little half-breed."

I got up and dusted myself off. Seems I'd spent most of this day getting knocked down by one bully or another.

"In my soccer game of life," I told Danny, "I just gave Goods the Red Card."

"I just gave him the finger," Danny said.

I decided not to tell my father about Goods hitting me with a full can of beer. My dad gets so excited about these things.

At dinner I said to him, "Did you ask Patrick?"

"Ask him what?"

"You said you wouldn't forget."

"Forget what?"

"That I wanted to go to the observatory."

"Oh. Yeah. Right."

"When will you ask him?"

"I already did. I just forgot to tell you. The answer is yes."

"When?"

"Tomorrow night."

My mother said, "That's Sunday. A school night."

"We'll go early," my father said. "There's no law that says you have to look at stars at three in the morning."

"Can Danny come?" I asked.

"Sure," my dad said.

"And Babcock?"

"Sure. Who's Babcock?"

"A new kid. And Dylan?"

"You can bring the whole soccer team if you want."

"Just one more. Geraldine."

My mother interrupted: "You know, Boone, maybe you should wait a week. You look so beat up with your eye and all, maybe you should go to bed early."

"I'm okay," I said.

"How's your back?" Danny asked.

"It's okay." I tried to signal Danny with my eyes not to mention the incident with Goods.

"What happened to his back?" my father asked.

"It ran into a beer can," Danny said.

"It *what*?" my father said. "Tell me *exactly* what happened."

So I had to tell him.

He didn't rant and rave, though, as I had expected. His face looked as hard as granite. "That does it," he said softly.

He scarcely said another word for the rest of the meal.

6.
The Trashathon

Sunday morning all eleven kids of the soccer team gathered at the lake. The ducks and the mean goose swam over to see if we had any food. They hopped around at our feet, quacking and fighting. The dogs came around, too, but they kept their distance from the goose.

Walt had gotten a scale and a big blue Dumpster. He had a clipboard for recording our hauls. He gave each of us a garbage bag, then raised a pistol. It wasn't exactly a starter's pistol. It was a Smith and Wesson 44 Magnum.

"On your mark, get set, *garbage*!" he shouted, and fired the pistol into the air.

The ducks took wing. The goose pecked Walt in the leg.

We each took a different street. I, of course, had

to take Pinecone Way, Danny's street, because of my promise to Meyer Tate. If I picked up garbage from any other street, it would only be worth the ten cents a pound that my father had pledged.

One of the dogs came along with me. He was a brown mutt with one ear hanging down and the other poking straight up.

In front of Danny's house at the bottom of the hill, I found two bubble gum wrappers. Twenty feet farther up, I found a bottle cap. For thirty feet more, I found nothing.

The mutt was searching just as hard as I was. He couldn't find anything, either.

Meyer Tate had beat me, but good.

I said to the dog, "Why don't you knock over a couple of garbage cans?"

The mutt cocked his head and stared at me.

I looked back down the hill toward the lake. Already, some kids were bringing full bags back to the Dumpster. Walt would weigh them, note the amount on the clipboard, and give them a fresh bag.

The ducks had returned and were checking out the garbage. The goose, meanwhile, had taken a strong dislike to the scale. Maybe he thought it was a big metal bird. He kept nudging it, honking and twisting his neck.

Jack Bean was driving around in the Beanstalk in case anybody's bag got so heavy they couldn't carry it.

I walked on. I found a plastic straw. I looked up

toward the top of the hill and saw Meyer Tate smiling back at me from behind his gate. He waved, like we were old friends.

I sat down on the edge of the ditch next to the road.

It just wasn't *fair*.

I kicked my foot against the side of the ditch. A clod of dirt fell loose. The brown dog with the up-and-down ears got interested in the fresh earth I'd exposed. He crouched, sniffing. Then he dug. The dirt flew backward from his paws between his hind legs and onto my lap. I saw something. Metal. Rusty. I pulled the dog aside, kicked again, and another clod fell away.

It was a link of chain.

I kicked, and dug with my hands, and the mutt dug with his paws, and soon I pulled out a rusty six-foot chain. It was heavy. I looked up the hill and held out the chain for Tate to see.

He nodded. Ten bucks, he was probably thinking. He could certainly afford that.

I put the chain in my bag and continued up the hill. The dog followed. I found an aluminum poptop, a plastic six-pack binder, a small bolt — and I had reached Meyer Tate's gate at the top of the hill.

"How you doing?" he said cheerily.

"You cheat," I said.

He frowned. "That's a serious charge," he said. "I broke no rules. I'm a man of honor."

The dog growled.

"That your dog?" Tate said. "He looks dangerous. You should put him on a leash."

Walking down the hill on the opposite side of the street, the mutt and I found a lottery coupon with all the numbers scratched off, a cassette cartridge with about a quarter mile of tape curling out of it, a post-card advertising a drapery cleaner, and one more bot-tle top.

At least I'd found the chain.

I walked over to the scale and handed my bag to Walt.

He refused to take it. "Don't hand me that bag," he said. "It's empty."

"I can't *find* anything," I said.

"Go back and try again," he said.

Even the ducks showed no interest in my bag.

Dylan came walking down to the lake, rolling an old tire. Walt weighed it: forty pounds.

The goose was now courting the scale, strutting and dancing.

I took my bag and sat down in front of Danny's house. I was so mad, I took the chain out of the bag and started whipping it onto the dirt. *Whomp.* A cloud of dust scooted away as it hit the ground. The dog scampered to a safe distance.

Whomp. Whomp. Whomp. Clang.

I'd hit the bumper of one of the old cars in Danny's yard.

Jack Bean was driving around, checking on how

everybody was doing. I looked at the Beanstalk. Those huge tires. I looked at Danny's yard. Two cars. And in the yard of the cabin up the road, one more.

I looked at the chain in my hands.

I ran for Jack. The dog ran at my heels.

"I've got something that won't fit in my bag," I said. "Could you give me a hand?"

"That's what I'm here for."

He backed the truck into Danny's yard. We looped the chain from the rear of the Beanstalk around the bumper of an old Packard. Then we climbed into the cab.

Danny's father came out on the porch to watch. In the darkness behind the window, I could see the shy eyes of Emma peering out.

Jack shifted down. "Granny gear," he said. "Granny granny."

Burbaroom. Burbaroom.

He let in the clutch. The truck jerked, halted, jerked again. *Burbaroom.* The engine grunted and roared. Suddenly, the Packard broke free from twenty years of dirt and vines and fallen leaves and started sliding along across the yard and onto the street. The mutt chased after it, barking.

Standing in the street was Meyer Tate with his hands outstretched.

"Stop!" he shouted. "That's cheating!"

Jack stopped.

I leaned my head out the window. "That's a serious

charge," I said. "I broke no rules. I'm a man of honor."

"Those are *my* cars," Tate shouted. "I *forbid* you to move them."

Danny's father walked down from the porch. He had a limp.

"Tate," he said. "You gave me those cars. Remember? When I moved in here, you said, 'They're not my cars. They're yours. You can sell them if you want to.' Everybody knows that."

"Show me your bill of sale," Tate said.

"Show me yours," Danny's father said. "You can't. Because they're nobody's. They're *garbage*. And that's what these kids are collecting. What's your stake in this, anyway? Did you actually make a pledge to this boy Boone?"

"No," Tate said. "Not that I can remember."

I pulled the pledge card out of my pocket. "Remember this?" I said.

"How much was the pledge?" Danny's father asked.

"One cent," Tate said, and he looked at me with pleading eyes.

I felt sorry for him. To tell you the truth, I actually wanted to let him off the hook.

Jack Bean snatched the card out of my hand. "It says here," he called out, "one dollar and one cent per pound. Signed, Meyer B. Tate."

Danny's father clapped his hands and cackled with joy.

Tate's shoulders slumped. He turned and walked

up the hill toward his house without a backward glance.

It was his own fault, I told myself. If he hadn't been so cheap as to collect all the trash before I could get it, I never would've gotten so desperate as to think of removing the cars.

Jack Bean and I hauled three cars — saplings, wasp nests, pine needles, blackberry vines, worms, and all — to the lake. They plowed small furrows in the asphalt as he dragged them. The brown dog followed, barking, darting at the cars and then jumping back. I think he thought he was herding them, like cows.

Walt's scale was large, but not *that* large.

"We'll have to estimate," Walt said.

"Hold it." It was Danny's father. He'd limped over from his house to watch the proceedings. In fact, quite a crowd had gathered. Word must have spread at the Pub.

Danny's father said, "We don't want to give Tate any room to quibble. I'll call Benny at the quarry."

Benny, the owner of the gravel quarry and no friend of Meyer Tate's, sent over a dump truck pulling a crane on a flatbed trailer. The ducks — and even the goose — retreated to the pond. About a dozen dogs gathered around. Danny's father operated the crane himself. He loaded the cars into the truck and drove back to the quarry where they had a truck scale.

All the soccer team and most of the parents — including mine — were waiting when the dump truck returned. Danny's father climbed down and announced the results: nine thousand, three hundred and twenty-six pounds.

Everybody cheered.

Walt began stroking his beard.

"We're going to need a treasurer," he said. "Somebody to keep track of all this money. And to help collect it. Boone, here, may need some assistance, for example. Any volunteers?"

Walt looked out at the members of the soccer team and their parents. There was a movement, and Emma, who I hadn't even known was there, shy Emma with her gloves and bangs, stepped out from behind the dump truck. "I will," she said.

I saw Walt look at Emma and narrow his eyes. I saw my dad do the same. In fact, it seemed every man there got a peculiar look on his face when he saw Emma. I think I'd be shy, too, if people always looked at me that way.

Emma, meanwhile, wouldn't look anybody in the eye. She stared hard at the ground. I had to wonder why she volunteered. She must've known it would put her in the spotlight. I thought it was great, though, that she wanted to help, just as it was great that Danny's father had helped by calling the quarry and operating the crane. Maybe there was hope for Danny's family after all. Maybe Danny's dad was ready to come off the bench.

"Excellent," Walt said. "You're on."

First, I went over to my dad and told him he owed

me ten cents times nine thousand, three hundred and twenty-six pounds.

"Do I get a discount for prompt payment?" he asked.

"No," I said.

"Family discount?"

"No."

"Student discount?"

"You aren't a student."

"Senior citizen discount?"

"No. And you aren't that old."

"I'm old enough to know the value of nine hundred and thirty-two dollars and sixty cents," he said. But then he brought his checkbook out of his pocket and wrote me a check.

"Who do I make it out to?" he said. "Australia?"

Walt said, "Make it out to the Thunderbolts. Emma, you'll have to open a bank account in the name of the Thunderbolts."

She nodded shyly. She looked like she wanted to hide. Everybody was eyeing her. In broad daylight. She put her hand to her head and tried to sweep more hair down over the scar on her face.

I was thinking, if it's this hard to get this much money out of my own father, how hard will it be to get ten times as much out of Meyer Tate?

I was glad I had somebody to help, even if it was only Emma.

She walked with me up Pinecone Way. The brown mutt followed. He seemed to have adopted me.

Emma's chest jiggled when she walked. It gave me
a funny feeling, and I didn't want to stare, especially
knowing how shy she was, so I dropped back a step
and walked behind her.

Her bottom jiggled, too.

I stepped fast until I was up in front of her, and I
stayed that way until we reached Meyer Tate's.

I had to help Emma climb over the gate. Her hand
in its glove squeezed mine. "Don't let go," she said,
and she jumped to the ground — and jiggled all over.

I knocked on Meyer Tate's door.

Nothing happened. Not a sound. I knew he was in
there.

I pounded on the door.

At last, it opened.

He looked surprised to see Emma there.

"Good afternoon, Mr. Tate," Emma said.

Tate swallowed. "Uh. Yes," he said. "Good —
um — afternoon." He looked down at me. "What do
you want?"

I opened my mouth, and once again I realized that
I hadn't planned what I wanted to say.

"It's . . . uh . . ." I said.

"Well?"

"I. I'm here. I want . . ."

"Can't you *speak*?"

I closed my eyes. I tried to gather all the facts into
words. When I thought I was ready, I opened my eyes
and said, "It's the Miserthon. I trashed your street.

Now we weighed it, and Emma is nine thousand three hundred and twenty-six pounds."

Tate glared at me as if I were a caterpillar on his rose bush.

Emma took a deep breath. "I'll handle this," she said. Her hands were shaking. "Mr. Tate, could I have something to drink?"

He looked at her crossly. But then he couldn't seem to look away. He held the door open and stepped aside.

Emma walked in.

I took a step forward, and Tate slammed the door in my face.

I sat on the steps of the porch. I saw where a line of bees was flying to and from a hive, making honey in Meyer Tate's apple tree.

At last the door opened. Emma walked out, adjusting a glove. And between her fingers, she held a check.

Tate said, "Now you just be sure to give credit where credit is due."

"Yes, sir," Emma said. "We will, Mr. Tate."

Together we walked down Pinecone Way. The brown dog had waited for us at the gate.

"Did Tate actually pay the whole thing?" I said.

Emma nodded.

"Did he try to weasel out of it?"

She nodded again.

"But he paid. Right?"

She nodded.

"What did he mean about giving credit where credit is due?" I asked.

"He wants everyone to know that he donated all this money. He wants everyone to think he's some kind of nice guy."

"I bet he's a better person than we give him credit for," I said.

"He's a creep," Emma said. "A rich creep."

Without another word, Emma turned and walked across Danny's yard and into the house.

Out of the house ran Danny. "Hey Boone. Did you get it?"

"Emma got it."

"Wow."

"Yeah."

"I collected all my money," Danny said, and he took it out of his pocket and showed it to me: two twenty-dollar bills, a ten, and three ones. "Hardly seems to matter now, does it?"

"It all helps," I said.

"Maybe Emma's all right," Danny said. "She hates Meyer Tate. She wishes he was poor, and she was rich."

"Everybody wishes they were rich," I said.

"Not like Emma wishes it. She hates being poor. She just *hates* it. You know what she does? She watches those game shows on television, and she clenches her fists, and she kicks the wall when people win those prizes. She wants one of those two-week cruises on the Caribbean."

"She should try to get on one of those shows."

"Emma? On television? Not her. The scars and all. She'd never do it."

Just then, Emma poked her head out the door. "Danny," she said. "You collected your money yet?"

"Right here," Danny said, and he jogged over to the door and reached into his pocket. "Here you are."

"Forty-three dollars?" Emma said.

"That's right," Danny said.

I didn't say anything. I just turned and ran home. The mutt ran at my heels.

7.
Phobos
and a Blue Light

"Tonight's the night of the observatory," my father said. "I didn't forget."

I wished he had. I'd invited Babcock, Dylan, Geraldine, and of course Danny, whom I didn't want to see just now.

We met at the lake. I walked down with my dad. The brown mutt with the one ear up and one ear down had waited for me outside the house. He bounced up when he saw me and tagged along as we walked.

The last sunlight had just disappeared from the tops of the hills, and now all was shadow below and lingering light above. It's always been my favorite time when the last bustle of day pushes up against the beginning magic of night. I said so, once, to my parents. My father said I was a budding romantic with a capital R. My mother said I was simply a poet. With, perhaps, a capital P.

Which I'm not — either one. I'm a kid. With a small k.

We passed the abandoned Studebaker that my dad had been so interested in. Goodey wasn't there, but I saw a sleeping bag draped over the back seat and some bottles and cans on the dashboard. The dog wandered over and peed on a tire.

Babcock, Geraldine, and Danny were already there at the lake. To nobody's surprise, Dylan was late, so we had to wait. Danny and Geraldine got into a rock-skipping contest. Babcock just stood looking out over the pond. I tried to see what he was seeing. Some swallows were skimming over the water. A bat came darting over our heads. The ducks were all roosting in the low branches of the trees at the edge of the water.

"Where do the dragonflies go at night?" I asked Babcock.

"They sleep," he said. "They latch on to a weed."

That seemed strange to me, the idea of an insect sleeping. "Do they snore?" I said.

Babcock laughed.

"Do they curl up in a ball?" I asked.

"They just sit there like an airplane that's been parked. They can't fold their wings."

"Do they *dream*?"

Babcock looked startled. He put a finger to his lips and seemed to be thinking. "I don't know," he said after a few moments. "That's a good question."

"If you were a dragonfly, what would you dream about?"

Babcock answered without any hesitation and with his eyes to the sky. "Soaring," he said softly.

I tried to imagine the fat body of Babcock swooping, diving, and soaring in the air over the lake and the trees and the grass. And right then, I thought maybe I knew why he was so fond of dragonflies.

Dylan came racing up to us on his bicycle. He skidded to a stop, leaped off the bike and in the same motion without warning tackled Geraldine to the ground. Geraldine had been in the midst of throwing a skipping rock. She tumbled to her side, rolled over once, and jumped on top of Dylan. After just a few seconds of struggle, she had her knees on his shoulders. She's a foot taller than Dylan and many pounds heavier.

"What did you tackle me for?" she said.

"I dunno," Dylan said. "Would you let me up?"

Geraldine looked to Danny and said, "What are we gonna do with this guy?"

"Let's sit on his face and fart on him," Danny said.

"Let's go to the observatory," my father said.

Geraldine reached down and mussed up Dylan's hair, then stood up.

Dylan has a crop of hair that's second only to Geraldine's. He always carries a comb in his back pocket. Now he looked annoyed. "What'd you do that for?" he said.

"For tackling me," she said.

"I was only being friendly."

"So was I."

Dylan walked beside Geraldine, combing his hair with one hand and pushing his bike with the other. He's the best dresser among us, and he always keeps his hair combed. He likes to think he's one sharp-looking dude, which he might be if he didn't pull dumb stunts like tackling Geraldine. Now he had dust all over his turtleneck shirt and trousers.

Lately, I'd noticed, Dylan had been giving a lot of attention to Geraldine.

Babcock walked beside my father.

I found myself walking beside Danny. I concentrated on dribbling a small pinecone as if it were a soccer ball.

Danny said, "So what's bugging you?"

"Nothing," I said because that's what you always say to that question, and then I gave the pinecone a vicious kick. The dog ran after it and fetched it back. In a low voice so nobody else could hear, I said, "You stole ten dollars from the Trashathon."

"Oh," Danny said. "That."

"Yeah. That."

"Well, it was only Emma. Whenever she sends me to the store, I don't give her the change unless she asks for it. Usually she doesn't. And if she does, I hold something back. That's just how we do things."

"It's stealing."

"Hey. You've got your house. And I've got mine."

And there it was again: that other planet, that parallel dimension where Danny lives.

"She'd do the same to me," Danny said.

"She would not," I said. "Grown-ups don't steal from *kids.*"

Danny looked at me with surprise. "Wanna bet?" he said.

"Yeah."

"How much?"

"A billion dollars."

"Okay." Danny laughed. "It's a bet."

Danny grabbed my pinecone from the dog's mouth and kicked it himself. "I'll give her the ten bucks. Since it's for the team. Except I bought some Milk Duds. And a grape soda. But I'll give her the rest. And then when you pay me the billion dollars, I'll even pay her for the Milk Duds and soda."

The observatory was a small white dome on a hillside above Patrick's house. Patrick was a big, broad-waisted man with a white mustache and red suspenders. He built the observatory himself, and the telescope, too. He even ground the mirror himself into a parabolic curve. He showed us how he did it.

"Are you an astronomer?" Geraldine asked.

"Mailman," Patrick said. "Retired. This is just a hobby. I'm a comet watcher. Do you know what that is? I search for new comets. There're hundreds of people like me. Every once in a while, a new comet that nobody has ever seen before appears in the sky. The first person to find it gets to name it."

"Do you get any money for it?" Danny asked.

"No," Patrick said.

"Have you ever found one?" Danny asked.

"No."

"How long have you been looking?"

"Five years."

Danny shook his head. "Five years," he muttered. "For *nothing.*"

The sky was just getting dark.

"There's a star," Dylan said.

"Actually, that's not a star but a planet," Patrick said. "That's Mars. And if we look at it through the telescope, we might be able to see one of its moons."

"How many does it have?" I asked.

"Two. They're quite small. The biggest is less than twenty miles from one side to the other. That's only as far as from here to Pulgas Park. If you took this mountain that we're standing on the side of, and lifted it into the sky, you'd have a moon about the size of Phobos. It's like a big floating boulder, really. Shaped like a potato. But you won't be able to see its shape with this telescope. Now, I can only fit two or three of you at a time inside the observatory, so you'll have to take turns."

Dylan and Geraldine took the first turn. My father went into Patrick's house to read a magazine. When Dylan and Geraldine came out, Danny, Babcock, and I all squeezed inside.

Mars was red. The moon — Phobos — didn't look like a potato or like the mountain that we live on the side of. It was just a tiny sparkling point of light that happened to be fifty million miles away. But I liked it. Usually when people start talking about astronomy, they throw out all these huge, unbelievable numbers about how big and distant everything is. But Phobos sounded just my size.

Next, Patrick focused on Saturn. We three each took turns looking at its rings and some of its moons. Patrick said one of those moons was made almost entirely of ice. Then we stepped outside so Dylan and Geraldine could have another turn — and couldn't find them. There was just the brown mutt looking up at me and wagging his tail.

"Dylan! Geraldine!" we shouted into the night.

We checked inside to see if they had gone in the house with my father. He said no.

Patrick said, "It looks like the only stars that interest Dylan are the ones he sees in Geraldine's eyes."

My father said, "Good grief! Was I supposed to be their *chaperone*?"

We returned to the telescope. Now the sky was fully dark. We looked at the Crab Nebula. Then Danny said he wanted to see a black hole.

"You can't," Babcock said. "That's the whole thing about a black hole. It's *black*."

Just then we heard barking outside. We looked out, and there was Dylan — covered with blood — like one of those movie shots after the guy with the ax has gone on a rampage through the motel. Which

scared the bejesus out of us for a moment. I thought
somebody had slit his throat.

"Got a Kleenex?" Dylan asked. "I seem to have a
bloody nose."

Babcock handed him a handkerchief.

"Where's Geraldine?" I asked.

"She went home," Dylan said. "She — uh — she
got kinda mad."

"Mad at what?" I said.

"Me."

"Did you tackle her again?"

"No."

"Did you do something to make her mad?"

"I guess so. I kissed her."

"Does that have something to do with the fact that
you now have a bloody nose?"

"I guess so. Yeah."

Patrick said, "You must have kissed her mighty
hard."

"It wasn't the kiss," Dylan said. "It was afterwards,
when she punched me."

Patrick shook his head. He said, "How can the
wonders of the heavens possibly compete with the
wonders of a boy and a girl?"

To me it was no contest. I'd rather look through
Patrick's telescope than mess around with Geraldine
any time.

My dad came out of the house, sized up the blood
on Dylan's face and shirt, and said, "Looks like Ger-

aldine doesn't need me for a chaperone. But you, Dylan, next time you go courting, maybe you should bring along a bodyguard."

"Hey," Babcock said. He pointed to the sky. "What's *that*?"

"Where?" Patrick said.

"There," Babcock said. "That blue light. Hey. It's *moving*."

"Where?" Patrick said.

"Oh yeah," I said. I saw it.

"Dsh, yeah," said Danny.

"Right there," said Dylan.

"Where?"

"There!"

"I don't see anything."

"Look where we're pointing."

"Do you see it, Tom?"

"No, Patrick."

It was a bright blue, unblinking point of light. It was moving slowly but steadily across the sky. All the kids could see it. And neither of the grown-ups could.

Babcock said, "It's crossing Cassiopeia."

Patrick and my father stared hard.

It was as bright as the brightest star.

"If it's moving," Patrick said, "it must be a satellite. Or a jet."

"But can you see it?"

"No."

"It's a UFO," Danny said.

"Nonsense," Patrick said.

"How do you know?" Danny said. "You can't even see it."

"It's a satellite," Patrick said.

Babcock said, "If it's a satellite, why is it blue?"

"I don't know," Patrick said. "It must be a jet."

Babcock said, "Jets don't have blue lights."

"The atmosphere must be refracting the light," Patrick said. "The same way it makes the air look blue."

"It's a UFO," Danny said, "and only kids can see it."

"Baloney," Patrick said.

"It's probably got kids for the crew," Danny said. "They're watching us right now. The reason you can't see it is because they don't want you to. They just want the kids to see it. All over the *world,* man. They're watching out for us. They're like our *body-guards.*"

At that moment, standing on that hill in the dark with a few lights of town winking through the trees below us and a billion stars over our heads, I was ready to believe what Danny was saying.

I felt creepy and wonderful at the same time.

I felt like we kids stood alone and apart from the crazy messed-up world of grown-ups. And yet we were not alone because somewhere, something that grown-ups are blind to, like that bright blue point of light slipping silently, slowly across the sky, was watching out for us. It would *help* us somehow. To do something. To make a better *world* some day, a world with rules as simple and goals as clear as a game of soccer. A world that was *fair*.

I awoke in the night in my bed. I'd been dreaming of Phobos. I could hear my father leaving the house. The clock over my bed said 3:14. I shut my eyes and went right back to sleep.

I slept poorly. I heard sirens. Then it must have quieted down because I was dreaming again.

The next sound I heard was the ringing of the telephone. It was 5:35.

I was just drifting back to sleep when my mother came into my room and turned on the light. She looked worried — in fact, she looked scared.

"Boone," she said. "I have to go to Pulgas Park right away. You'll have to help me. Is your alarm set?"

"Yes."

"What time?"

"Six-thirty."

She was furiously brushing her hair as she talked. She held a hairclip between her teeth. She said, "I want you to be awake when Dale and Clover get up. You're in charge. See that they get dressed and have breakfast. I don't know when I'll be back."

She put the clip in her hair.

"All right," I said. "What was that phone call?"

"That was Tom." My mother put her hand on my shoulder. "Puerco Pub burned down last night. It was arson. Your father was arrested. They caught him walking the street at four in the morning carrying a half-empty can of gasoline."

I sat up. "You mean he's in *jail*?"

"Yes, Boone. Your father is in jail."

8.
Flake

Sleep? No way.

I followed my mom to the kitchen door. When she opened it, I saw the brown dog with the one lop-ear curled up on the doormat. He picked up his head and batted his tail on the redwood decking.

My mother stepped over him without a word. I think she was too upset to even notice he was there.

It was still mostly dark.

I watched my mom's taillights go down the road between the tall trees. I'm in charge, I thought. I'm responsible for the whole house until she comes back. I'm — almost — the *father*.

For my first act as boss of the house, I looked in the refrigerator, found some old sloppy joe sauce in a plastic dish, and set it out on the porch.

The dog leaped to his feet.

In two seconds, the sauce was gone. The dog looked up at me and wagged his tail. With the light pouring out of the kitchen door, I could just barely see our garbage can by the road. Still upright.

"Good dog," I said, and I scratched his ears. I tried to make the floppy ear stand up, but it collapsed as soon as I let go. It was creased across the middle.

I needed someone to talk to. Having the dog for company was a small help. Here it was six o'clock in the morning and my father was in jail. My brother and sister were sleeping. They didn't even *know* about it.

My dad had wished for a meteorite to blow the pub to smithereens. I guess he got impatient, waiting.

How could he do it? He's not a violent person. Sometimes he gets angry, but then he cools off. He never hit me, for instance, and I've made him plenty mad sometimes.

How many years do you get for arson?

There's a prison right outside of town. Every day, a white van with bars over the windows goes down the highway through San Puerco, bringing prisoners or taking them away. Would my dad be in that van today? Would I be a grown-up before he got out of jail? Would he stay in that prison right out of town? I might be the substitute father for *years*. Would I have to quit school, go out and get a job? No. I was too young.

Oh no. *School.* Everybody would *know*.

Wait. I can't go to school. I have to stay home and take care of Dale. At least until my mom comes home.

I poured myself a bowl of cornflakes and tried to eat them. I love cornflakes. This morning, though, for some reason they tasted like mushy old newspaper to me. I mean, they tasted the same as always, but I wasn't in the mood for food, I guess, so they seemed like newspaper.

I put the bowl outside the door.

The single-lop-eared dog devoured every last shred of cornflakes and then kept licking the bowl. He liked it even better than the sloppy joe sauce. With each slurp, his tongue pushed the bowl a few inches across the porch until it had traveled all the way to the steps — where it fell and broke into three pieces — one of my mother's favorite ceramic bowls. And still he was licking one of the pieces. I had to take it away from him. I was afraid he'd cut his tongue on the sharp edge.

We'd need a dog now to help me guard the house.

I went back inside the kitchen and, just out of curiosity, filled up another bowl, unbreakable plastic this time, with cornflakes. I added no milk. I set the bowl outside the door.

The dog gave a yip of joy. He actually pounced on it. He crunched. He slobbered. He snuffled. Saliva drooled in strings from his lips. Cornflakes stuck all over his snout and whiskers. He finished the bowl and then licked his tongue in a circle around his mouth. Out of reach of his tongue, cornflakes hung on his ears and eyebrows. He sat, looked up at me, and thumped his tail.

"Whatcha doing?" It was my sister Clover. She was barefoot, wearing a nightgown, holding a fuzzy toy bear.

"Feeding the dog," I said.

"Where'd he come from?"

"He's been following me."

"Dogs *always* follow you. You're a dog *magnet*."

"I can't help it."

Clover shifted the bear in her arms. "What's his name?" she said.

"Um. Flake."

"Flake?"

"Flake."

"Is he *yours*?"

"He seems to think so."

"Did Daddy say you could keep him?"

"Um. No. I haven't asked. Yet."

"Let's go ask."

"He isn't here."

"Let's ask Mommy."

"Um. She's not here."

"Where are they?"

"Um. Pulgas Park."

"Volvoville?"

"Yes."

I hoped she wouldn't ask what they were doing there. I didn't want to be the one to explain that Dad was in jail. I hoped my mother would come home soon. Until then, I planned to tell Clover that there wasn't any school today.

My little brother Dale shuffled into the kitchen. He was wearing a sweatsuit. He wore them day and night. He was scratching his belly. "Where's Mommy?" he asked.

"Volvoville," Clover said.

"Where's Daddy?"

"Same place," she said.

Dale thought it over. He said, "Are they buying a Bulbo?"

"*Volvo,*" Clover said.

I said, "He'll never buy a Volvo. He says we're Volkswagen people. And maybe he's also a Studebaker person."

Dale said, "Don't say that."

"Why not?"

"Don't call Daddy a stupid baker."

"*Studebaker,*" I said. "It's a kind of old car."

"Oh." Dale continued to scratch his belly. "I'm hungry," he said.

"What do you want?" I said. "I'll fix it."

"Envelope," Dale said.

"A *what*?"

"I want an envelope."

"What for?"

"For breakfast. Make me an envelope."

"He means omelet," Clover said.

"I don't know how to make an omelet," I said. "How about some cornflakes?"

"Awful," Dale said.

"I thought you liked cornflakes."

"Awful."

"I guess you changed your mind."

"*Awful*. I want a awful."

"He means waffle," Clover said.

"Oh," I said. Usually I can understand Dale. This morning I guess I was distracted. "I don't know how to fix waffles."

Dale looked disappointed. He stopped scratching his belly, looked up at me, and said, "Can you cook bipsips?"

"Bipsips?"

"Biscuits," Clover said.

"No," I said.

"Can't you cook *anything*?" Dale asked.

"Cornflakes," I said.

"Never mind," Dale said, and he went to the refrigerator. "I'll just get some rorgut."

I looked at Clover.

"Yogurt," she said. "And I want some, too."

This must be how it feels to be a grown-up, I thought, talking to kids who you can't understand, who ask for things you can't give them, and meanwhile you're keeping secrets from them because you don't know how to explain.

"Is school today?" Clover said.

"No," I said.

And *lying,* I thought.

About ten o'clock in the morning, I heard our Volkswagen bus parking on the street. I looked out the door. Down the path to our house I saw my mother walking, and to my surprise right beside her was my father. He looked tired and rumpled. In his hand he was holding some papers.

I threw open the door and ran to them. The dog, Flake, who had been curled up on the doormat, came running after me, barking and bouncing. I threw my hands around my dad and hugged him, and he hugged me back. His shirt smelled stale, like cigarette smoke and something else, like urine. I wondered if that was the smell of jail.

"How'd you get out?" I said. "Did you *escape*?"

"Of course not," he said. His hand holding the papers was shaking.

"Then how — "

"On bail," he said.

"What's that?"

"Money."

"You mean you can pay to get out of prison?"

"No. Well. Sort of. You see you can — "

"Dad. Why'd you do it?"

He looked surprised. "Do what?" he said.

"Burn the Pub."

His face got very serious. He stooped down so that he was level with my eyes. "Boone," he said, "I didn't do it."

"Didn't they catch you with a can of gas?"

"Yes." He scratched his face. He needed to shave. "That's the problem. I couldn't sleep. As usual. So I took a walk in the moonlight, and there was that old

Studebaker. I thought I'd do something useful. If bringing that old wreck to our house can be considered useful. I went back home for a gas can, and I put some gas in the tank — "

"But that's Damon Goodey's *house*. Wasn't he there?"

"Nope. Just his empty bottles. And an empty sleeping bag."

"Where else could he be at three in the morning?"

"Probably off stealing something. Anyway, I put some gas in the tank, but it still wouldn't start because I'd forgotten the battery was dead. I was walking back to the house when I heard the sirens. I could see the fire all the way from that corner of the road right over there. I walked down to see what was going on. And they arrested me."

"And that's — that's *true*?"

He looked annoyed. "Of course it's true."

I remembered being in a similar situation myself. "Word of honor?" I said.

"Word of honor," he said.

"Then I believe you." It felt good to say that. In fact, it felt *great*.

My father looked relieved. He stood up. "What's this dog?" he asked.

"That's Flake."

"Who does he belong to?"

"Well," I said, "he thinks he belongs to me."

"No," my father said.

My mother said, "Tom, let's talk about this some

other time. You should get some sleep."

"Fine," he said. "But first, I want to throw out that other can of gas from the garage. I'll pour it in the car. That stuff is *dangerous.*"

As he left, I said to my mom, "Do the police still think he did it?"

"Yes," she said. "And I can see their point. They don't know Tom. And his alibi sounds pretty far-fetched."

"So what's going to happen?"

"There'll be a trial. We have a lawyer. There'll be a judge and a jury. We'll have to convince the jury that your father is telling the truth."

"What if we don't?"

"We will."

"But what if they don't believe him?"

"Don't you believe him?"

"Of course. He gave me his word of honor."

"Then so will they."

"But what if — "

"Boone," she said. "Don't ask."

I guess what she meant was, *don't ask me.* I couldn't help asking myself, *what if my father went to jail?*

My father took a shower and went to bed — at ten-thirty in the morning.

My mother said Clover could stay home for the rest of the school day. But I should go, she said, and be the family's "front line."

"Why me?" I asked. "Why not her?"

"Because you're older."

"That's not fair."

"I can't change the fact that you're older. Can you?"

"No."

"Sometimes being older is an advantage. Sometimes it's a pain. The older you get, the more you'll become aware of that. It's not a question of fair."

"Walt says life isn't fair."

My mother frowned. "Maybe it isn't," she said. "But we try to make it as fair as we can."

Usually I walk to school, but this time my mother drove. We passed what was left of the Pub: a brick chimney and a pile of black charcoal. About a dozen people, the regulars, were standing around the wreckage. One of them was Danny's father. He saw our bus and made a gesture with his arm that was not of a friendly nature.

Now it wasn't just Damon Goodey who hated me. It was half the town — the drinking half. And once again, it was for something I didn't do.

"What'll they do without a bar to go to?" I asked.

"Drink at home," my mother said.

"Will they rebuild it?"

"I don't know. It belongs to Meyer Tate."

"Miser Tate? He won't spend a penny on it."

"He will if he sees a profit in it. He won't if he doesn't."

At school every face turned to stare at me as I

walked into the classroom. My mom whispered a few words to Mrs. Rule, who pursed her lips and nodded her head.

I sat down. My desk was at the back of the room. Every face was turned around to look at me.

"Now class," Mrs. Rule said. "We were talking about square roots."

Nobody looked at her.

"Ladies and gentlemen," she said, which she only said when she was getting angry.

A few heads turned toward her, but most stayed looking at me. Though nobody said anything, I could hear the question ringing loud and clear.

"He didn't do it," I said.

"What?" said Mrs. Rule.

"My father didn't do it. He didn't start the fire."

Mrs. Rule said, "We are not going to — "

"They caught him with a can of *gas*," Danny said.

"It was an accident," I said.

"Oh, yeah," Danny laughed. "He just *accidentally* poured gasoline on the Pub and *accidentally* dropped a match onto it."

"He just happened to be in the wrong place at the wrong time," I said.

"*Dsh*," Danny said, spreading his arms like an exploding ball of fire.

"Ladies and *gentlemen*," Mrs. Rule said.

I stood up. I leaned forward over my desk toward all the silent faces. "He gave me his word of *honor*," I said. "And I *believe* him."

Mrs. Rule stared at me with an expression that was just one notch softer than The Look. "Do you wish to make a speech?" she said.

"No," I said, and sat down.

"Now, class," said Mrs. Rule. "Square roots."

Dylan asked, "What do the police say?"

I said, "They don't believe him."

"Is he in *jail*?" Geraldine asked.

"No."

"Why not?"

"All right, class," Mrs. Rule said. "I see it's time for a lesson in civics. Go ahead, Boone. Tell Geraldine — tell all of us — why your father isn't in jail."

"He paid money," I said. "To get out."

"And what is that money called?"

"Bail."

"And can anybody do that? Can people buy their way out of prison? Is that fair?"

"I don't know," I said.

"Does anybody know?" Mrs. Rule asked.

Babcock raised his hand.

"Bail is for before you go to trial," Babcock said. "You pay the money as a promise that you'll show up at the trial. If you don't, you lose the money."

"Right," said Mrs. Rule. "Because you're innocent until proven guilty. And if you're innocent, you shouldn't be in jail. After the trial, if you're guilty, then you can't buy your way out and you have to go to jail."

"If you're black," Babcock said.

"If you're *anything*," Mrs. Rule said.

"If you're black, you go to jail," Babcock said.

"Or brown," Danny said. "But if you're white, you pay a fine."

"That's not fair," I said. At the same time I was sort of glad to hear it. Maybe, I thought, even if they find my father guilty, they'll just make him pay a fine.

"It isn't true," Mrs. Rule said.

"It is true," Babcock said. "*You* should know. I got an uncle who — "

"Just last night," Mrs. Rule said, "on the evening news I saw a man sentenced to twenty years for robbing banks. He's white. And he's in prison now, and he'll be there for a long time to come."

"But that was *big*," Babcock said. "That was on television and everything. I'm talking about the little guy. The guy who shoplifts or something. My uncle went to jail for speeding in Mississippi. They wouldn't put a white man in jail for that. Especially if he's rich."

"What about a rich black man?" Mrs. Rule said. "Would he go to jail?"

"No," Babcock said. "Probably not."

"Then is the problem money? Or race?"

Babcock thought a moment. "It's both," he said. "More white people are rich. And if a white man is poor, he still has a better chance to stay out of jail. That's what my uncle said."

"Well, then, if you think it's true," Mrs. Rule said, "what are you going to do about it?"

"Nothing," Babcock said, and he leaned his chin on his fist.

"Why not?"

"I can't."

"Why not?"

"I'm just a *kid*."

"Do you want to do anything about it when you grow up?"

"I can't."

"Why not?"

"You can't beat the system."

Mrs. Rule frowned. "Did Martin Luther King say that?"

Babcock thought about the question. "I guess not," he said.

"And thank goodness he didn't," Mrs. Rule said. "Or you might not even be able to sit in this classroom today. And I certainly wouldn't be able to teach it. You might not even be able to live in a house in this town. Things have changed. *He* changed them. *He* didn't think you can't beat the system. And he beat it."

"And he got shot," Babcock said.

"Yes, he did," Mrs. Rule said. "And did shooting him stop any of the changes he helped to make?"

Babcock shrugged. "No. I guess not."

"Are you afraid, Babcock?"

"Some."

"Don't be. That would mean that everything Martin Luther King worked for was wasted. It would mean that shooting somebody would kill not just the man but the spirit as well. It would mean that the world will never get any better. Can you kill a spirit? Do you like the world the way it is?"

Babcock knew what Mrs. Rule wanted him to say. So naturally he didn't say it. "Some," he said. "I like dragonflies."

"I mean the human world. The world where black people are more likely to go to jail than whites."

"No."

"If you don't like the system, if something isn't fair to you, go out and change it. Maybe alone you don't have power, but if enough of you feel the same way you can act together. You can change the world. That's your job. You are the future. And my job is to teach you that. If you learn only one thing from my class, if you take just one bit of knowledge into the rest of your life, I want it to be that you have power. You are the future. You can make it *fair*."

For a moment, everyone was silent. I think everyone sat up a little taller in his or her seat, reflecting on Mrs. Rule's little speech.

Then Babcock raised his hand.

"Yes, Babcock?"

"You mean, Mrs. Rule, if we know that, we don't have to learn square roots?"

Flake met me walking home from school. He brought along five of his friends. I was just walking along, alone, and suddenly I was surrounded by dogs.

Flake came up and rubbed his muzzle on my knee. Then he walked along at my side. The other dogs followed. That is, they ran circles, barked, jumped in and out of the duck pond, dashed off into the bushes and dashed back covered with brambles and burrs, scratched their ears, snapped at flies, rolled in dirt, sniffed at trees, and brought their three-ring circus along at my general pace. None wore collars.

I walked to Danny's house. He wasn't in his yard. The whole place looked empty with all the old cars removed. Nothing had grown back yet to cover the ground.

I didn't want to knock on his door. His father might answer, and I didn't want to encounter him after the gesture he'd made at us that morning. So I kept on walking up Pinecone Way. I was thinking about something that happened at school. At recess, some kids had yelled at me, "Burn the school! Next time, burn the school!"

At least, Danny and Babcock and all the kids in my class seemed to believe me. Well, maybe not Danny.

At the top of the hill a voice interrupted my daydreaming.

"You!" It was Meyer Tate. "Are these your dogs?"

"No," I said.

Three of the dogs were in his yard. Another was wiggling under his wire fence. One had already started to dig a hole in his garden.

"I'm calling the pound," he shouted. "This is Dogville! I swear! The last sound I hear in this life will be that of a barking dog. Of that I am absolutely sure. So what do you want? You think you can get more money?"

"No. I'm . . . just walking. Um . . . Mr. Tate?"

"What?"

"Are you going to rebuild the Pub?"

He laughed. It sounded like a horse's whinny. "Am I crazy? There's no profit. That bar has lost money for years. The insurance will pay me twice what it's worth. I'm going to use that money to tear down an empty house that I own and build a new one and sell it. Now *that's* profit."

Just then, he noticed that one of the dogs had completely unearthed a young rosebush. "I'm calling the dogcatcher," he said, and stomped toward his house.

It was just as Tate had bragged to Babcock and me when he made his pledge for the Trashathon: He knew how to use a deal to his own advantage. Except the Trashathon had backfired on him. Which was his own fault, for trying to be such a cheapskate. But the fire insurance would make up for it; in fact, it would probably make up for it ten times over.

I walked back down the hill. Flake saw me go and ran to my side. Another dog ran yipping at his heels. The dog who had been digging looked up with a nose covered with dirt. He bounded to the fence and squeezed under on his belly. Within a few minutes, all the dogs were out of Tate's yard and following me in their own doggy way.

All my life, it seems, dogs have followed me. And when they haven't, I've followed them. The thing I like about dogs is that they always show their feelings. No surprises. They don't hide anything the way cats do — cats and people. Dogs have rules, and all dogs know them, and if people know them they can get along just fine with dogs. Dogs are *fair*.

When I returned home, the dogs were still following me. I stood on the deck by the door, watching to see what they'd do. The sun was going down. Redwood shadows spread over the house mixed with shafts of sunlight. Everything was letting go of its colors, turning richer, deeper, darker.

Flake lay down on the doormat. The other dogs spread out in the yard. I saw one go over to the garbage can, get up on his hind legs with his front paws on the lid, and give it a sniff. Flake ran up and growled him away.

Good dog. Good watchdog. Or, perhaps Flake wanted to save the garbage for his own plunder. But he hadn't tipped it last night.

My father opened the door and came out where I was standing. "Good grief," he said. "How did we get six dogs in our yard?"

"They followed me," I said.

"No," he said.

"Yes. They followed me home."

"I mean, no. You can't keep them."

"Only one."

"Which?"

"This guy. His name's Flake."

"How do you know his name?"

"I named him."

"Boone. We've been through this before."

"Yes. We have." A blue jay was hopping along a rail of the deck. From the low branch of a nearby tree, a squirrel was chattering at the jay. The squirrel had a raggedy tail, as if something had chewed on it. I heard the hoot of an early-rising owl. All the sights and sounds were familiar. I'd heard it all, seen it all, a hundred times before. I knew that the jay would turn around and squawk at the squirrel with the raggedy tail — and a moment later, he did. I felt older — much older — than yesterday. I said, "You always say I can't keep a dog until I'm old enough to take care of him entirely by myself. Which I am. Dad — I was the father this morning. You were gone. I give you my word of honor. I'll take care of this dog."

My father reached down and tried to straighten Flake's one floppy ear. As soon as he let go, it bent.

Then he looked me directly in the eye. "I'll take your word of honor," he said. "Just as you took mine."

He held out his hand.

It took me a moment to realize what he wanted. Then I grabbed his hand and shook it. "Deal," I said. "Wait here. I want you to see something." And I ran to the kitchen for a plastic bowl and a box of corn-flakes.

Flake dived into the meal like an Olympic swimmer.

In half a minute, every cornflake was gone except for one that had lodged in his nostril and that he was trying to sneeze out.

"I'm impressed," my father said.

"And he's a watchdog," I said. "He'll guard us. We need that, now."

"We don't need a guard dog."

"We *do*. Half the town *hates* us."

"Who?"

"The drinkers."

"I didn't burn the Pub. They'll find that out."

"When?"

"When they catch the guy who did it."

"What if they never catch him? What if they aren't even looking because they think you did it?"

"Do you really think they hate us, Boone? Has anybody said anything?"

"At school. Some kids. And Danny's father didn't say anything, but he went like this." And I made the gesture with my arm.

My father laughed. "I haven't seen that since Italy," he said.

"It's not funny."

"Boone. Believe me. All your life you're going to run into people who try to make you feel bad. If not for this, then for some other reason. They'll tell you your ears are too big or your nose looks funny or you're wearing the wrong clothes or your father is an idiot. Or a criminal. They'll *test* you. It makes them feel big to make you feel small. But it's just a test to see how strong you are. How strong of mind. Of character. And *you* have to pass that test. Some dog can't pass it for you."

"How do I pass?"

"By sticking to your word. And by showing them that they can't make you feel bad because you know who you are and what you stand for."

I looked out at the yard. All the dogs had disappeared in darkness — except Flake, who had sneezed the cornflake out of his nose and now lay on the doormat at my feet. I saw Mars, a bright point in the sky. Next to Mars I imagined I could see Phobos — not the real Phobos, the cold bare rock in the sky — but a Phobos in my mind, a soft mountain of a moon covered by trees and deer and squirrels with dragonflies flashing over a pond, and there'd be little people who lived in a little town a lot like ours with woodsmoke curling from the chimneys and a soccer team that always played by the rules. "I know who I am," I said. "But what do I stand for?"

"What's important to you, Boone?" my father asked. "How do you want the world to be?"

Like Phobos. My Phobos.

"Fair," I said.

"Attaboy," my father said. "And you know what? I like this dog."

9.
The Tree

The next morning I started walking to school by myself with my lunch in a bag. Flake followed. As I passed the duck pond, the pack of five dogs joined in.

Down at the corner of the lake where the teenagers like to park their trucks and haul logs and goof around, I saw a different truck. It was white, with rows of little doors that had bars over the windows.

The dogcatcher.

Tate had called him.

What I did next wasn't a decision because I didn't even have to think about it. I just did it. I turned around and walked the other way.

The dogs followed.

I walked up the road to the dead end and continued on the foottrail into the woods. The dogs were delighted. All around me dogs were dancing through

111

the bushes, playing tug-of-war with sticks, digging at tunnels, flushing a rabbit, and barking at a bird.

I walked way back to where there's a little creek that drops to a pool. I sat on a root sticking out of the bank, ate an apple from my lunchbag, and thought about what I was doing. I was missing school. I was keeping five dogs from the pound. I could wait an hour, then go late to school after the dogcatcher had given up and gone away. I'd be in trouble for being late, but it wouldn't be too bad.

I skipped stones across the little pool.

I started noticing the different personalities of the dogs. One was a runner, lean and tall. She could fly, and she loved to go charging down the trail, then turn and race back again just for the joy of it. One was a hunter, short and fuzzy, with his nose to the ground. He kept dashing into the weeds and flushing out quail or rabbit or mice. One was goofy, lanky, jumpy, always trying to start a game of fetch. One was a swimmer, chasing my pebbles across the pool. One was shy, spooky, always at a distance. And Flake seemed to be mostly a guardian. He stayed near my side, and he growled if any other dog came too near either to me or my lunchbag. I guess partly he was guarding and partly he was possessive. Jealous.

After an hour, I led the dogs back down the trail to the road. They followed me into town. I was heading toward school when I walked around a streetcorner and suddenly found myself not ten yards from the dogcatcher's truck. He was talking to Meyer Tate.

They saw me. And they saw all the dogs.

Have you ever seen a flock of birds scooting across the sky in tight formation when suddenly, on some secret signal, each and every bird at the exact same moment changes direction, and the flock heads off in the same formation? That's how it was with me and the dogs. I turned and ran. Each dog, whatever he'd been doing, turned and ran with me.

The dogcatcher ran, too. And Tate ran after the dogcatcher.

Tate dropped off after one short block.

The dogcatcher kept running. He was bigger than me, but all those laps Walt made us run plus all the running of a soccer game had built my legs into pretty good shape. I made it past the lake. My lunchbag tore open, and food flew every which way as my arm pumped up and down. One of the dogs grabbed my sandwich from the ground and ran along with it in his mouth.

I huffed up the road and onto the trail. About a hundred yards into the woods, I slowed to a walk. I'd beaten him. I knew he wouldn't follow me here. All the dogs were with me, tongues hanging. I was still holding the empty, torn paper bag.

So we returned to the little pool.

I'd noticed as we were running that the hunter dog had a limp. He had a head like a terrier and a body like a beagle. I coaxed him, cooing, into letting me examine his leg, but I couldn't see anything wrong on the outside.

I examined the other dogs. They were all crawling with fleas. Fat ticks hung like grapes on their flesh. The swimmer, a tan dog with a bent tail, had a sore on his shoulder that was oozing pus.

I was in trouble now. The dogcatcher knew I was hiding the dogs, and Tate knew my name.

I was hungry.

There was a giant redwood growing near the pool, and a younger tree — a sucker — was growing out from the base of the big tree. I climbed up the branches of the sucker until I could reach the bottom branches of the big tree twenty feet above the ground, then I switched over to the big tree and climbed up and up and up. When I came to a break in the branches, I sat down and looked out across the woods. The hill sloped down, so I could see half the town from here. Flake sat at the foot of the tree, panting. The other dogs wandered around.

I was a bird.

I could see Danny's house, the lake, my house, the chimney of the Pub, cars crawling slowly along the roads, and below me I could see anybody in the forest long before they got near me. Away from town I could see the prison and its fences, the gravel quarry, and the hills sloping from green to gray to the fog out over the ocean, ten miles away.

I wanted to come back with boards and build a fort.

I wanted to have binoculars so I could really be a spy. I wanted to store food up there, and maybe even sleep there.

For now, though, I couldn't do anything. I had to stay. I could see the dogcatcher's truck like a matchbox car, still parked where I'd almost walked into it.

After about an hour, I saw the truck drive away. It disappeared into a hollow. I couldn't tell whether it had left town or only moved to a different street.

The sun rolled slowly across the sky. A hawk soared in lazy circles. Little birds — chickadees — flew in busy, noisy bunches from tree to tree, sometimes below me, sometimes above. A crow was cawing, somewhere.

I looked down and realized that the dogs had all wandered off. Only Flake remained at the base of the tree.

I climbed down. As soon as Flake saw that I was coming, he started to dance. He leaped against the base of the tree, barking a yowly sound like a police siren, and jumped up as if he were trying to meet me halfway. Then when I reached the ground, he ran a big circle around me and the tree, and then shot off into the forest. A minute later, he reappeared at my side, calmer now, and we walked home together. It was time for school to let out.

I got home just before my sister. I waited outside, and when she came walking up the road I ran to her.

"Where were you today?" she asked.

"Don't snitch," I said. "Just don't say anything."

"Why?"

"I was hiding the dogs from the dogcatcher."

Her eyes got wide. "Did it work?"

I looked around. "I don't know," I said. I couldn't see any dogs except Flake. But I hoped they were somewhere around town, that they hadn't wandered back only to find the dogcatcher still waiting. I didn't think he could wait all day. He must have other dogs to catch.

"I won't tell," Clover said.

"Cross your heart?" I asked just as she was saying, "Cross my heart."

"Jinx," I said.

"Forget jinx," she said, and she held out her hands with her pinkies extended. "Here. Hook your pinkies with mine."

"Why?"

"To get a wish, silly. You can wish the dogs are safe. Come on."

So I hooked my pinkies with hers.

"What goes up the chimney?" she said. "Say smoke."

"Smoke," I said.

She swung her arms, crossing them first over and then under each other, and my arms swung too because our pinkies were still hooked.

"My wish and your wish will never be broke," she said as we swung our arms. Then she let go. "There. Now you get your wish."

"Does that really work?" I said.

"Not very well. What works better is holding your breath while you pass a church. Or if you drive through a tunnel, holding your breath all the way through with your finger in the air. Your right pointer."

"I've seen you do that. And you do that for cemeteries, too."

"You don't get a wish for graveyards. You hold your breath so you won't get a bad dream. And railroad tracks. When you drive over railroad tracks, you have to pick up your feet off the floor or you'll get hit by a train."

"I didn't. And I didn't get hit."

"You will. It doesn't happen right away."

Great galloping banana slugs! As if I didn't have enough problems, now my little sister says I'm going to get hit by a train.

"I don't believe it," I said.

"You'll be sorry," she said.

That evening, I kept expecting the phone to ring. Meyer Tate, or the dogcatcher, or the school, or the police — *somebody* — would call. After all, I'd skipped school, interfered with the dogcatcher, and been seen by Meyer Tate.

I was so nervous waiting for that phone that instead of watching where I was walking, I blundered right through the toy town that my little brother Dale had built out of blocks on the living room rug. He'd been constructing an elaborate railroad station. The depot fell on the wooden tracks and broke up the whole train. Dale said, "Hey! Snotnoodle!" and he grabbed the engine and threw it — and hit me in the ear.

"Ow!" I said. "You didn't have to do that."

Clover laughed. "I warned you," she said. "I told you you'd get hit by a train."

The phone never rang.

The next morning my dad left for work, my mom left to run errands with Dale, and Clover and I — and Flake — left for school. Down at the lake, we picked up the five stray dogs.

Good. They'd made it.

I saw a tow truck hooking up the old abandoned Studebaker. My father had missed his chance. And Damon Goodey would have to find a new home. I didn't see his sleeping bag. I guess he'd already found one.

Then I saw the dogcatcher's truck. It was far enough away that I didn't have to panic. I simply turned and walked the other way. Flake — and the five strays — followed.

I stopped at my house on the way to the woods, used the key we keep hidden under a flowerpot, and let myself in. I took my father's binoculars, a pair of tweezers, and a tube of first-aid cream. Then I walked the dogs back to the creek and the little pool. I wondered, how many days will that dogcatcher keep coming back? And how long can I get away with this?

All my life it had seemed that everybody always knew everything I was doing. Suddenly I found that I could take a whole day off to go sit in a tree, and *nobody noticed*.

It was wonderful. Nobody controlling me. Nobody telling me what to do. I was free in my tree.

It was also scary. I mean, *who's watching out for me?*

I rubbed first-aid cream into the oozing sore on the shoulder of the tan dog with the bent tail. It made him nervous, but he let me do it, and afterward he gave my face a complete washing.

I pulled ticks off every dog, even the shy one. They trusted me. They liked me.

I decided to buy a can of flea powder at the grocery after school let out.

I climbed the tree with the binoculars around my neck and my lunchbag tucked under my shirt so I could keep both hands free.

From my perch, I could see the whole world. My world, at least. Phobos.

The dogs started wandering away. From my lunchbag I took out the potato chips and dropped them one at a time to the ground, like falling snow. The dogs chased them, tried to snap them in the air, fought each other to grab them off the ground. It kept them nearby for a while.

Looking out over town, I couldn't see the dogcatcher's truck anywhere. Either he'd left town, or he was hidden from my sight in a hollow or behind some trees.

The dogs were getting restless. I broke my tuna fish sandwich into small bits and dropped each bit, one by one. I threw them in a circle. The dogs would smell one bit and rush over to it, and then I'd throw another bit on the opposite side of the tree, and they'd smell it and dash over there.

Now all I had left was an apple and a candy bar, which the dogs wouldn't want. So I ate them. The dogs sat around near the tree, hoping for more.

After a while, they started wandering off. By that time I felt pretty sure that the dogcatcher had given up and gone away. I could climb down and go to school for the remainder of the day.

But I didn't.

Showing up late at school would only point out the fact that I'd been missing. What could I say?

Besides, I wanted to sit on this branch with my back against the trunk and learn more about my wonderful little moon. I could read the land below me like a map. There was the highway leading to the beach. There were the narrow, twisting little streets of San Puerco. There was a farm road on the other side of the valley and, near me, a forest road — just a fire trail — that nobody ever used. A couple of years ago, somebody found a body at the end of that forest road where an animal had dug it out of a shallow grave. They thought it had been murdered, but it had lain there so long, nobody could tell for sure.

Through the binoculars I watched trucks being loaded at the quarry. I saw cars parking in front of the little grocery store and itsy-bitsy post office that are all there is to downtown San Puerco now that the bar's burned up. I saw a man repairing a roof. I saw down into a fenced yard where a woman was taking a sunbath without any top on. I saw cattle in a field way up on a hill. I saw individual prisoners walking behind the chainlink fence of the prison, and I tried to guess what each man was in for. My father said it was a minimum-security prison — that's why there's only a chainlink fence with some barbwire on top — where they send the least dangerous criminals, the ones, he said, who rob with a computer, not with a gun.

Suddenly I became aware that I was not alone. On a branch less than ten feet above and to the side of me sat a red-tailed hawk. He must have flown in from behind my back or I would have seen him coming.

I froze.

The hawk, too, was motionless. His talons were immense. His beak looked sharp as a knife. He was staring out over the land just as I had been doing. Oddly, seeing him so close, he looked scruffy, as if he were a schoolkid slouching behind a desk. His feathers seemed ruffled, tousled, like hair that needed combing.

As he looked around, his eyes moved toward where I was sitting — and stopped. He was staring right into my eyes.

I was trying to keep still, but I felt a shiver run down my spine.

I met his stare. For a few seconds. Then I had to look away. His eyes were stronger.

When I looked again at him, he was gazing out over the land below.

Then suddenly his eyes locked onto something. He sat up erect. Now every feather fell into place. He was magnificent. He spread his wings with a rustling sound and was just lifting off the branch, getting ready to dive on some rodent, when from out of nowhere a small, dark-colored bird plunged silently out of the sky and smashed into the hawk's back. A couple of pieces of feather floated out in the breeze. The bird scooted away and above the hawk, who looked completely surprised — and annoyed. The little dark bird flew about twenty feet higher than the hawk, tucked in its legs and wings, and dropped like a missile.

Smash!

More feathers flew.

Now the hawk was angry. He flapped his wings and flew higher, but the little bird was quicker and knew to stay above and behind the hawk.

Another dive. Smash! The hawk staggered in its flight.

I was amazed. I've seen mobbing before where a

whole flock of little birds gangs up on a hawk or an owl and chases it away, but here was one lone little bird taking on a red-tail five times his size. I thought of my last soccer game, how Walt had matched me up against number One. It's like that in the real world, too, the world outside of soccer. The dogcatcher was the hawk. I was a sparrow. And I could fly circles around him.

Now the red-tail was beating a retreat. It set out for the trees on the other side of the valley with the little bird chasing and diving in pursuit.

I watched with the binoculars. The hawk wasn't trying to defend itself anymore, but was flying directly away when the little bird tried one more dive — and missed. It glanced off the side of the red-tail and dropped below. In a flash the hawk cupped his wings to slow down, turned, and shot down toward that little bird.

Caught.

The hawk clutched the little bird in his talons.

Slowly now, silently, the red-tail flapped his wings and flew to a tree on the other side of the valley. I stopped watching. I did not want to watch myself being eaten — ripped piece by piece — by the dogcatcher.

Tomorrow, I decided, I would see if I could get Danny and Babcock and maybe even Dylan and Geraldine to help hide the dogs.

There are good reasons why little birds fly in flocks.

* * *

That evening, the school called. So did the Humane Society. So did Meyer Tate, to report that five dogs which he had often seen with me had dug craters in his rose garden.

One question I hate to answer is the one that begins, "How could you possibly think — ?"

After two days in a redwood tree, I had to answer that question at dinner. Three times.

It's supposed to be the other way around. Here was a case of the hawks ganging up on the sparrow.

"It wasn't Flake," I told my mother and father. "It was his friends. At Meyer Tate's."

I promised that I would walk directly to school the next day and every day thereafter. I vowed that I understood the need for dogcatchers and the damage that a pack of stray dogs can do: they spread disease (rabies!); they have worms; they raid garbage cans; they kill livestock. Sometimes they even attack people! A pack of wild dogs might even *eat little children!*

I stated that I was very, very sorry, that I was ashamed, that I had reformed.

In other words, I lied.

The next morning I slipped my father's binoculars into my lunchbag along with a new can of flea powder. Flake and I walked down to the lake to recruit my sparrow friends and find the other dogs for a powder party and a day in the woods. Danny especially would love my tree. Babcock might have trouble climbing it. Forget school. We could build a fort. If anybody came after us, we could see them coming long before they arrived and vanish like foxes into the surrounding forest.

I walked around a bend coming to the lake, and Flake froze in his tracks. There was the dogcatcher, shutting a cage door on his truck — on the last stray dog. Five doors, five dogs. The man saw me. He frowned. Then he saw Flake. He grabbed his net and came running.

I turned and ran, not to the woods this time because the man was too close, but back to my house. I held my lunchbag from the bottom so it wouldn't fly apart.

The dogcatcher stopped at the edge of my yard.

Flake, beside me on the porch, growled.

"That your dog?"

"Yes," I said.

"I can't take him when he's on your property. But you better keep him there."

I made a barrier across the porch out of pieces of wood. Flake stayed. And I went to school.

I never saw those five dogs again. I could have called the pound to find out whether anybody had adopted any of them, but I didn't. I wanted to believe that they had all found a good home with a rug and a bowl and a bone.

My father said, "Do you remember, Boone, when I told you that the world would test you?"

"Yes," I said. "And I could pass the test by knowing who I was and what I stood for."

"Exactly," he said. "What I am just now realizing is that you also are testing the world to find out just who it is and what it stands for, particularly in the case of stray dogs and attending school."

"Maybe," I said.

"Did you get an answer?"

"Yes."

And maybe that's fair.

10.
The Picket Line

We won our next two soccer games. In fact, we didn't just win — we *dominated*, six to nothing and eight to one. Babcock took it as a personal insult if anyone on the other team dared to so much as try to score a goal. Danny and Geraldine passed to each other and punched in goals as smoothly as a machine.

Dylan was jealous of how well they worked together while he was stuck at fullback. Leaving his post one time, he ran forward and tried to take a pass from Geraldine. He muffed it, though, and the other team stole the ball and took it all the way down the field — where Dylan was supposed to be defending — and scored their only goal. Walt nearly tore out his beard. After that, Dylan stayed back.

Near the end of the second game, I had a collision with a blond-haired boy on the other team. Our legs tangled. We both fell down. I heard a crack like a broomstick snapping in half. I stood up again, but the other boy's leg bent sideways at the knee. Dylan took one look and vomited. They had to call an ambulance. The kid was writhing and screaming. When play finally resumed, the ref called a foul on me.

"We were both going for the ball," I said.

"I know," the ref said. "But I feel like I ought to call *something*."

I sort of agreed. If I ever break my leg in a soccer game, I'll want them to call a foul on somebody whether they deserve it or not, just out of respect for what happened.

Unfortunately, Danny's father did not agree. This was the first soccer game he'd ever attended — and I hoped it was the last. He'd been screaming from the sidelines ever since the first kickoff, taunting the other team, calling them names, and riding the referee. When the ref called the foul on me, Danny's father yelled, "That kid got what he deserved, the little punk. Are you blind? How much did they pay you?" Then he said eleven more words. The first was "You," the last was "mother," and the other nine shouldn't be repeated. I was impressed. I'd never heard somebody string nine cuss words together like that. Two of them I'd never even heard before, but I knew they were swearwords just from the sound of them.

The ref walked over toward the sideline. He was a big guy with powerful hairy legs bursting out of his black shorts. He looked like a buffalo. I heard he used to play on a pro team in Argentina. Danny's father, seeing the ref coming, started walking belligerently onto the field. He was small and wiry. Walt got a worried look on his face and ran out between them.

It was Danny, though, who saved the day. Before a fight could erupt — and, most likely, his father get squashed — Danny ran over and said, "Go back, Pop. It's only a soccer game."

His father seemed startled to hear Danny's voice. He snapped around, saw Danny, and smiled. "Hi, Danny," he said.

"Go back, Pop. This is a game. For kids. You have to stay on the side."

His father looked at the ref, acting puzzled, as if he was wondering what am I doing here? He made a wave with his hand, turned, and walked back to the side of the field.

"Keep him out of here," the ref said to Walt.

"I'll try," Walt said.

"I'm going to report this," the ref said.

Five minutes later, the game was over.

After each game, we get drinks from a cooler brought by one of the parents. Danny grabbed his drink and headed straight for the parking lot. He hopped into the back seat of Emma's old Chevelle. In the driver's seat sat Emma, wearing sunglasses, gloves, and long sleeves, and next to her was Danny's father.

Emma, of course, had been too shy to come out and watch the game.

The next day, I got a phone call from Danny.

"Guess where I'm calling from," he said.

"Somebody's house?" I asked.

"Yep. Mine."

"You got a phone?"

"Emma got it. And a big new TV set. She got a job at a video store in Pulgas Park. She's making *money*. She said to me, 'Danny, I ain't gonna be poor no more. If you want to have money, you got to go out and take it.' "

"You mean, make it."

"Yeah. I guess. Take it. Make it. Ain't it neat? You should come over and watch something."

"I'll be over."

"Not now," Danny said. "My dad's watching a war movie. Then Emma's got her game shows."

"Well, some time, then."

"Dsh."

At the next soccer practice, Walt arrived looking totally glum and disgusted. He called us together for an announcement. "The season's over," he said. "Forever. We won't play any more games. They dropped us from the league."

"How can they?" Babcock said.

"It's the middle of the *season*," Danny said.

"That's not fair," I said.

Walt gave me a pitying look. I knew his answer regarding the relative fairness of the world.

"That little blond kid who broke his leg," Walt said. "That was the son of the league president."

"Hey, I'm *sorry*," I said. "It was an *accident*."

"Also," Walt said, "the referee reported us for indecent and threatening behavior on the sidelines."

"Dsh," Danny said, and we all knew he meant his father.

"The league is run by Pulgas Park for the children of Pulgas Park," Walt said. "They only let us play because we have nowhere else to go. And they never minded before because we always lost. But this year we're winning, and we're winning big. And then that kid gets hurt, and Dr. Jefferson, his father, the president of the league, says we're a bunch of big bad boys from that tough town in the mountains beating up on the nice boys in the valley."

"And girls," Geraldine said, twisting a finger in her ball of hair.

"Sorry," Walt said. "Big bad girls, too."

"Thank you," Geraldine said.

Babcock said, "Is the decision final?"

"Yes," Walt said. "Dr. Jefferson just called me on the phone. He's going to send me an official letter in a day or so."

"So what can we do?" Dylan said.

"Nothing," Walt said.

"It's the system," Babcock said.

"Can we still go to Australia?" I asked.

Walt grimaced. "If we don't play, we won't be in any kind of shape for a trip like that."

For a minute we all stood around kicking the dirt, except for Babcock, who had put his hand to his chin and seemed to be lost in deep thought.

It seemed to me that the hawks didn't deserve to win this one. Not against eleven sparrows. I said, "Couldn't we promise that Danny's father won't go to any more games?"

"I tried that," Walt said.

"Did you explain how it was an accident?" I said.

"I tried. But the ref called a foul on you."

"He didn't *mean* it."

"He called it."

He had me there. It had seemed fair at the time, but now, like everything else, it was coming out wrong.

"This Dr. Jefferson," Geraldine said. "Where does he live?"

"Pulgas Park," Walt said.

"You have his address?"

"Yes." Walt flipped through his clipboard. "Right here. Oh no. What do you want to do, Geraldine? Throw stones at his windows?"

"Well. I was thinking of something else."

"Don't toilet paper his trees, either."

"Aw, nuts."

"And don't knock over his mailbox or stinkbomb his car."

"Wow." Geraldine's eyes lit up. "I hadn't even thought of that."

"Don't do anything to embarrass me," Walt said.

Babcock stepped forward. "The point is to embarrass *him*, sir."

"What do you mean?"

"Call attention to him, sir."

"Would you *please* call me Walt?"

"Yes, sir. We need to call attention to him, sir. And make people sympathize with us."

"How do you want to call attention to him, Babcock? Sit on him?"

"Sit. A sit-in. That's a good idea, sir."

"I'm not going to give you the address." Walt held the clipboard to his chest.

"Don't you trust us, sir?"

"No."

"Aw, Dad," Dylan said.

"You're too young," Walt said. "You'll only make the situation worse."

"How could it get any worse?" Dylan asked.

"They could arrest us," Geraldine said eagerly. "They could send us to reform school."

"We haven't done anything wrong," Dylan said.

"I mean, if we trashed his house," Geraldine said.

"Exactly," Walt said.

"We can be nonviolent," Babcock said.

"Just forget it," Walt said. "That's how you can be nonviolent."

"You think you can't beat the system, sir?"

"That's right. You think you can, Babcock?"

"I don't know, sir."

"I'm not giving you the address. And he's a doctor. His phone is unlisted."

With that, Walt tucked the clipboard into his belt, climbed onto his Harley, and rumbled away.

Jack Bean still had all the soccer balls in a big yellow net in the back of his truck. Babcock turned to him. "Do we practice?" Babcock said.

"What for?" Jack asked.

"In case we have a game Saturday, sir."

"Call me Jack."

"Yes, sir. It might work, sir."

"What's your plan?"

"Are you on our side?" Babcock asked.

"Of course I'm on your side," Jack said. "And I'm also on Walt's side."

"For this, you have to choose. Do you want us to keep playing soccer, or do you want to give up?"

"I'm with you," Jack said.

"Then it's simple," Babcock said. "You can drive us. We can fit in the back of your truck, with three in the front."

"Where?"

"He's a doctor, right? He's got an office somewhere. We'll just look it up in the phone book."

"We're gonna toilet paper his office?" Geraldine said.

"We can have a sit-in," Babcock said. "We sit down

in his waiting room and fill it up so there isn't any room for his patients."

"And then what?" Dylan said.

"Then he calls the police," Babcock said.

"And then we leave?"

"No. We stay. Then the police come and tell us we're trespassing and we have to leave."

"And then we leave?"

"No. We stay."

"And then what?"

"Then they arrest us."

"And *then* we leave?"

"No. We stay. The police have to carry us out."

"And then we go to jail?"

Babcock shrugged. "Of course."

"How does that get us to play soccer?" Dylan asked.

"Don't you know about civil disobedience?" Babcock said. "The way a sit-in works is, they keep arresting people until all the jails are full and they run out of places to put everybody. Then they have to let them go."

"There're only eleven of us," Dylan said.

I remembered how my father's hand shook, how his clothes smelled after he came home from the police station.

"I don't want to go to jail," I said.

"Me neither," Dylan said.

"Cowards," Geraldine said.

Babcock sighed. "It *is* a problem that there're only eleven of us," he said.

"Like you said, Babcock, it's the system," I said.

"Yep. Like I said." Babcock frowned. "Also, like I said, the point is to embarrass him. Hey. We could picket him. They don't arrest you for that."

"Picket how?"

"We make a line, and walk up and down, and carry signs."

"In his office?"

"Outside. So we aren't trespassing."

"Will that *work*?" Danny asked.

Babcock shrugged. "At least we'll be doing *something*," he said. "We can make signs tonight. Jack, can you meet us after school tomorrow?"

Jack nodded.

"Everybody in on this?"

We shrugged. We nodded. We muttered. We weren't exactly enthusiastic, but I guess we were curious as to what it would be like to be on a picket line. Anyway, nobody had the nerve to say no to Babcock. And it was better than doing nothing.

Jack Bean ran us through a short practice. Our hearts weren't in it, though. We were outcasts, and it hurt. Just because my legs had tangled with some kid, and Danny's father had gotten in a mood, and Danny had tried to steal a pocketknife, and people associated our town with the prison outside it and the rowdy bar that used to be within it, we weren't as good as them. We couldn't associate with them.

We were segregated. Discriminated against.

The more I thought about it, the more I liked Babcock's idea.

After practice, I had some extra time before dinner, so I took a walk with Flake to the woods. I climbed the tree to my lookout branch and settled back, scanning through my father's binoculars.

The sun was a fat red ball sinking behind a hazy ridge. Pink clouds rolled overhead. And in the prison yard, I saw one lone man wearing blue jeans and a gray sweatshirt. He was walking nonchalantly along the fence. I wondered, what had he done? How was he different from me?

Suddenly, just for a moment I saw my father standing behind that fence in that prison yard. It was so real, it scared me. Then, again, I saw it was the man in the gray sweatshirt.

I scanned across town. At Danny's house, I saw Emma reaching into the trunk of her car. Out of that beat-up old Chevelle she lifted a big cardboard box. It was heavy. She staggered as she carried it to the front porch. Another new television? I couldn't make out the writing on the box. She set the box inside the front door, then returned to the Chevelle and lifted another identical box out of the trunk. This time I could see the picture on the side of the box — a speaker. She'd bought a stereo system.

Near the pond I could see the goose waddling furiously out of the water across the hardened mud toward a man. I couldn't hear it, but I knew the goose was honking and hissing at the man — Damon Goodey. He threw a rock at the goose — and missed. He walked on. The goose stood indignantly honking at his back. I wished I could honk like that, honking *nyaa, nyaa, you missed me, now you've got to kiss me*. I watched Damon shuffle down the street. And I knew, watching him, that some day Damon Goodey was going to test me. I hoped, when it came, that I would be not a silly goose but a fast-flying sparrow whose aim was always true. Also, I hoped, I would just happen to be carrying a couple of hand grenades.

Lights were popping on in the windows of houses. With the binoculars I could see dinners cooking in the kitchens of San Puerco. I climbed down to the ground where Flake was jumping, dancing, leaping, and yowling like a siren, and then as soon as I touched earth he pounded a big circle around the tree and me and then boomed off into the woods. I walked away. A little way down the trail, Flake was waiting and wagging his tail, and together, home we walked.

I made a sign out of the side of a box of Arm & Hammer laundry detergent. I pasted white paper over everything except the picture of the arm and the hammer, and under the hammer I drew a picture of a little person looking like he was about to be smashed. Then in big letters I wrote, PLAY FAIR.

The next day after school under dark gray clouds, we all piled into the front and back of Jack Bean's pickup and drove over the hill to Pulgas Park. I'd been imagining some cozy little doctor's office where you walk right in off the street, but Dr. Jefferson's address turned out to be a six-story building in the middle of town. Jack parked in the underground garage, and we walked to the elevator carrying our little signs. I felt small.

We took the elevator to the lobby and got out and walked over to a building directory to find out which floor the office was on. A security guard spotted us right away. "Can I help you?" he asked.

"Yes, sir," Babcock said. "We're looking for Dr. Jefferson's office."

"What for?" the security guard said, eyeing our signs and looking like he'd just bitten into something rotten.

"To picket him, sir," Babcock said.

"You can't."

"Why not?"

"No peddling, solicitation, pamphlets, or petitions," the guard said.

"You didn't say 'no picketing,' sir."

"Read my lips," the guard said. "No picketing."

"It's a free country," Babcock said.

"It's a private building," the guard said.

We walked out the front door to the sidewalk. The clouds looked lower, darker, grayer.

"It's a public sidewalk," Babcock said. "We can picket here."

"That means we have to picket the whole *building*," Danny said.

"Got a better idea?" Babcock said.

"I feel stupid," Danny said. "Everybody's *looking*."

"That's what we want," Babcock said. "I think." He had a sign that said DON'T "KICK" US OUT OF SOCCER. He started walking down the sidewalk in front of the building. I fell in place behind him. Reluctantly, glancing at the people walking by us on the sidewalk, Danny joined in with everybody else.

One minute later, it started to rain.

Five minutes later, we were soaked. A couple of signs had been painted with waterbased paint. Now they looked like abstract art.

People dashed out of the building holding newspapers or shopping bags over their heads. They glanced at us, then hurried away.

One woman stopped. "What do you want?" she asked.

"We want to play soccer," Babcock said. "We were kicked out of the league."

"What for?"

"For breaking a kid's leg. And cussing from the sidelines. And we stole a kid's pocketknife, but we gave it back."

The woman's eyes grew large. She stepped back. "Well, I would kick you out, too," she said, and walked quickly away.

"Babcock," I said, "I think you'd better work on how you say that next time."

"I think you're right," Babcock said.

Dr. Jefferson probably didn't even know we were there.

The paste softened on my sign. The white paper peeled off. I was picketing with a sign that said ARM & HAMMER LAUNDRY DETERGENT. The cardboard was starting to curl.

A car pulled up to the curb beside us, splashing Dylan as it went through a puddle, and jerked to a stop. A police car. Blue lights flashing.

Two policemen got out of the car. The first thing I noticed about them was their belts. They each had nightsticks big as baseball bats, and pistols in holsters. On a rack behind the driver's seat was a big rifle with a wooden handle.

One policeman had a mustache. "What is this?" he said. "Sesame Street?"

"We're picketing," Babcock said.

"For what?"

"For soccer, sir."

"You got a permit?"

Babcock stopped walking. Raindrops plopped off his hair and streaked down his cheeks. "We need a *permit*?"

The policeman with the mustache got back into his car and started talking on the radio.

This is it, I thought. Now we're going to be arrested for picketing without a permit.

The rules to this game seemed totally rigged.

Just then a man in a white coat with a stethoscope dangling from his pocket came out the front door. A pin on his coat said DR. JEFFERSON.

"I want these hoodlums out of here," he said to

the other policeman. "This is harassment. Intimidation. They're *threatening* me. They'll start breaking windows next."

"They say that?" the policeman asked.

The policeman with the mustache stepped out of the car. "They don't need a permit," he said.

"They're underage," Dr. Jefferson said.

"I'm not," Jack Bean said. He'd been watching from a sheltered spot under an overhang.

"How old are you?" the policeman asked.

"How old do you want?" Jack said.

The policeman shrugged. He turned to Dr. Jefferson. "I think it's legal," he said.

A white van screeched to a stop behind the police car. EYEWITNESS NEWS, it said on the side. The two front doors flew open, the side door slid open, and two men and a woman jumped out. In ten seconds we were staring into the lens of a video camera held under an umbrella while a man in a powder-blue suit wearing a button that said CHARLIE quickly combed his hair and then stepped forward holding a microphone in one hand and an umbrella in the other. "Who's in charge here?" he asked.

We all looked at Babcock.

Babcock by this time looked like a coconut that had rolled through a carwash. He rubbed a finger over his glasses to wipe off the steam. "I guess I'm in charge," he said.

Charlie rushed over to him. "What's your name?"

"Babcock."

"What's your first name?"

"Babcock."

"Well, then, what's your last name?"

"Babcock."

"Wait. I thought you said — "

"Never mind."

"But — "

"Just call me Babcock."

"Oh. Well. Mr. Babcock, you can call me Charlie."

"Yes, sir."

"Can you tell me what's going on?"

"We're picketing Dr. Jefferson, sir."

"Who is Dr. Jefferson?"

"That man in the white coat. Running his fingers through his hair."

"Stewart. Get a shot of Dr. Jefferson."

Dr. Jefferson put his hands at his side. He looked as if he didn't know what to do with them. He smiled at the camera.

Charlie turned back to Babcock. "And why are you picketing this man?"

"It's our soccer team," Babcock said. "He told us we couldn't play any more."

"He did? Why not?"

"Because his son got hurt. He thinks it's our fault."

"And is it your fault?"

"No." With the rain streaking down Babcock's cheeks, it looked as if he were crying. "It was an accident. Sometimes people get injured. He fell down."

Charlie turned to his cameraman. "Stew, you getting all this? Isn't this *great*? Don't they look cold and miserable and bedraggled? 'Kids stand in rain for the love of soccer. Film at eleven.' "

"It's not that simple," Dr. Jefferson said.

Charlie walked over to Dr. Jefferson with his microphone. "Tell us, Dr. Jefferson. Tell Eyewitness News. What's your specialty, sir?"

"Pediatrics," Dr. Jefferson said.

Charlie's eyes lit up. We'd all gathered around him to hear what he'd say and also to get under the overhang of the building out of the rain. We dripped like wet mops.

"Here we have eleven children getting soaked in the rain, probably catching cold, Dr. Jefferson, risking their *health*, Dr. Jefferson, possibly coming down with *pneumonia*, Dr. Jefferson. They seem to really want to play soccer. Why can't they?"

Dr. Jefferson looked like a cornered animal. I felt sorry for him. He looked into the camera. He looked at Charlie. He looked at us. Softly he said, "My son's knee is shattered."

"It wasn't my fault," I said, and the camera turned to me and my curling Arm & Hammer sign. "We collided. We were both going for the ball."

"The referee called a foul," Dr. Jefferson said.

"He said he felt like he had to call something," I said. "If I had broken my leg, he would've called it on your son."

The camera turned back to Dr. Jefferson. Charlie

held a microphone to his face. We all waited.

"There have been incidents," Dr. Jefferson said. "There was swearing. There was a petty theft."

"He didn't *mean* it," Danny said, and the camera swung over toward him. "Sometimes he just gets *upset*. He *says* things. He can't help it. He won't do it again. And I gave back the pocketknife. We shook hands."

Standing next to Danny, I started to shiver. I was so cold, I couldn't help it. I was shaking uncontrollably. I looked up, and the camera was pointed right at me, taking it all in. So was Dr. Jefferson.

"This is all a misunderstanding," Dr. Jefferson said. He put his hands in his pockets. "I spoke to their coach on the phone." He took his hands out of his pockets and put them behind his back. "I was upset. I said some things." He looked at Danny.

Danny nodded.

He looked at me.

My teeth were chattering so loudly, I'm sure the microphone was picking up the sound.

Dr. Jefferson moved his hands to his side. "I haven't done anything yet." He folded his arms across his chest. He looked out over our faces. "I have patients waiting." He unfolded his arms and dropped his hands as if he'd given up on figuring out what to do with them. Then he looked directly at Babcock. "You have a lot of courage, coming here." Now he was looking right into the camera. "These children can continue to play soccer."

We all cheered.

With that, Dr. Jefferson's shoulders relaxed, his hands went into his pockets looking like they really belonged there, and he said, "Why don't you come into my office so I can give you some towels? My nurse can get you some hot chocolate."

Smiling to show all his teeth, Charlie spoke into the microphone: "This is Charles Wilson for Eye-witness News."

In the elevator on the way up to Dr. Jefferson's office, Babcock whispered to me, "Nice shivering. That was *brilliant*."

"I wasn't faking," I said. And I sneezed.

Geraldine patted her pocket and looked disappointed. "I guess I won't need this stinkbomb," she said.

11.
The Detective

I was sick for the rest of the week. By Saturday I felt better, but not well enough to play soccer, so I missed the game. Saturday afternoon, I walked over toward Danny's house and found him sitting by the lake, flipping pebbles into the water, looking gloomy.

"How was the game?" I asked.

"We lost. Forfeit. Missing three players. They all got sick from picketing in the rain." Danny studied me. "You look all right."

"I'm all right." I sat down beside him. "Maybe it's good that we lost a game. For the league, I mean."

"Maybe."

"What's wrong?"

Danny kicked at a root. "We been evicted," he said.

"What's that?" I asked.

"*Evicted*. It means the landlord kicks you out."

"Meyer Tate?"

"Dsh."

"He kicked you out of your house?"

"Not yet. But he told us we have to leave."

"When?"

"Thirty days."

"He can't do that. It's your house."

"He owns it."

"What'll you do?"

"My dad says we ain't leaving."

"Can't they make you leave?"

"I dunno."

"What will you do if they make you leave?"

"Leave."

"Where will you go?"

"Oklahoma."

"Then you won't be on the team! You won't go to Australia!"

"Is that all you think about? Soccer?"

"No — but — what are you going to do?"

"Nothing," Danny said, and he tossed another pebble into the water.

"I don't want you to go to Oklahoma," I said.

"Dsh" he said, and he looked at me with a halfway smile, which was his way of saying, thanks for saying you're my friend.

"Why don't you move to another house around here?"

"Can't afford it."

"But Emma's got a job now."

"She has to make payments on all the stuff she's buying. It ain't paid for yet."

"Maybe your dad could get more work at the quarry."

"He can get all the work he wants."

"Well then, that's great, he can — "

"He don't *want* it." Danny kicked at the root again. "Boone, don't you know *anything*?"

"What do you mean?"

Danny didn't answer. He just stared at me, and I looked back at him across the planet. If my life on Phobos was surrounded by trees and dragonflies, Danny's moon was larger, colder, uglier, maybe like that moon of Saturn that's made entirely of ice.

"Maybe it's the Banana Effect," I said.

"What's that?" Danny said.

"Something my father calls the Banana Effect. Things come in bunches. We lose the soccer game. You're being evicted. What next?" I flipped a pebble into the pond, and ripples started spreading in a circle.

Danny flipped another pebble into the center of my circle, and a new band of ripples began. He said, "Maybe an airplane will crash in the middle of town."

"Maybe there'll be a plague," I said, flipping another pebble, keeping up a continuous band of ripples. "We'll all die of a horrible disease. Everything will die. Except the banana slugs. They'll crawl over our dead bodies. And *eat* us."

"Naw," Danny said. "There's gonna be a nuclear

war. Somebody's gonna reach for a cup of coffee, and his elbow's gonna accidentally hit the button, and . . . ka-boom!"

"Wanna do something?" I said.

"No." Danny grinned. "Let's just sit here and be miserable all day."

So we went and explored the abandoned house on the lot next to Danny's. If Danny's house was on the verge of collapse, the one above it was beyond the verge. The last tenants had moved out several months earlier. The door wasn't locked. In fact, it wouldn't even close. The ceiling of one of the rooms had caved in from water damage. Wires were dangling in the air. Squirrels and rats had covered the floor with nuts and weeds and droppings. And in one corner, surrounded by empty bottles and cans, was Damon Goodey's sleeping bag.

"Tate's gonna tear it down," Danny said. "Then he's gonna tear my house down, too. He's gonna build two brand new houses. And *sell* them. He'll make a *million dollars*."

Danny picked up a board and smashed a window.

"Hey! Don't!" I said.

"He's gonna tear it down anyway," Danny said. "Come on. Grab a board."

"But Damon Goodey's moved in here. He must be living here, now."

"So what? You think he's *paying* for it?"

"No . . . but . . ."

Danny smashed another window.

"Take *that*, Miser Tate!" Danny yelled. *Smash*. "Take *that*, Damon Goodey!"

I picked up one of Goodey's empty bottles and felt its weight in my hand.

Danny moved on to the next room. *Smash*, I heard. *Smash. Smash.*

Without making up my mind to do it, without even thinking, simply letting my hand make the decision for me, suddenly I turned and threw the bottle as hard as I could across the room and against the wall. *Smash*.

It felt good. It felt *great*. I picked up another bottle.

We smashed every window and broke every bottle in the house. We kicked holes in walls. We tore the doors off the kitchen cabinets and ripped the shelves out of the pantry.

When we finished, the house looked as if a hurricane had hit it. Damon Goodey's sleeping bag was buried under plaster and glass and dust. And we felt like a million dollars.

Danny and I walked down to his house and started kicking a soccer ball around. It was almost supper time. I heard the goose honking at somebody, and then I saw Damon Goodey walking up the street.

As I watched from Danny's yard, Goodey pulled open the door of the abandoned house — and just stood there, staring inside. Then he turned around and saw me watching. And that's when I realized that Danny had disappeared.

"You!" Goodey shouted. "Did you do this?"

I didn't answer. I looked around for Danny.

"I'll *get* you for this," Goodey said, and he went into the house.

I walked over to Danny's porch. There was Danny, crouching behind a refrigerator that was lying on its side with the door cut off.

"Thanks for the help," I said to Danny.

"Hey. I ain't stupid," he said.

Goodey came back out of the house carrying his sleeping bag. He shook it out in the yard, making a cloud of dust as little bits of plaster and glass flew off into the weeds. He glared at me. Slowly he bent down and picked up a rock. He wound up, kicked his leg — and fired.

I dodged. I could hear it sizzle. It bounced off the side of Danny's house.

That man could still throw.

Something I just realized: In Damon Goodey's world, you don't get bawled out or sent to your room. You get hurt. Danny had already known — he knew all about Damon Goodey's world. A world not far from his own.

Goodey walked away with the sleeping bag under one arm.

Danny stayed where he was — behind the refrigerator.

Some time during Saturday night, I heard my father go out.

Sunday morning, the phone rang before anybody

was out of bed. I got up and answered it.

"Hello, Boone." It was my father's voice.

"Aren't you home? Where are you?" Then I remembered hearing him go out during the night. "Are you with Patrick?"

"I'm at the police station."

I fetched my mother. She talked to him, then told me the news: Another house had burned down last night. My father had been walking back from Patrick's observatory. He'd stopped to see if there was anything he could do to help, and they'd nabbed him.

"Which house?"

"The one above Danny's house."

My first thought was, did Danny and I do something to set that fire? But the electricity was shut off. The gas was disconnected. I didn't see how we could have caused it.

"So are you going to bring Dad home now?" I asked my mother.

"No, Boone." She shook her head. "He isn't coming home any time soon."

"What about bail?"

"They're holding him without bail."

"They can't do that!"

"They can if they think he'll commit another crime while he's out on bail."

"So he's going to stay in jail?"

"Today, at least. Tomorrow is Monday. Our lawyer may be able to arrange something then. We'll just have to wait and see."

"That was stupid!"

"He hasn't done anything wrong."

"But it *looks* wrong! Two fires! Both times he's there! In the middle of the night! One time he's even carrying a can of *gasoline*!"

"There's no law that says he can't look at a fire. Anyway, he thought he might be able to help."

"He's in *trouble*."

"Yes, Boone. He's in trouble."

"Will they put him in the prison that's right outside of town?"

My mother shook her head, but she didn't speak. She couldn't. She was crying.

I took a walk with Flake. For a moment I had felt like crying myself, but then some other feeling swept into my body: My head was clear, as clear as thoughts ever get, as clear as in that moment when you're in front of the soccer goal and the pass is coming toward you, the goalie is rushing out to you, and a couple of fullbacks are bearing down behind you, and somehow your brain goes into a special state where it can be aware of where all those people are — click — and meanwhile judge the speed and angle of the ball — click — and tell your foot just where to aim — click — and like magic, you score a goal. Or, if your brain is just the slightest bit distracted, you flub it.

Without even being aware that I was doing it, I walked into the forest and climbed my tree. Sitting on my special branch, with the whole town and hills below me and a cloud above that was exactly the shape of an elephant with trunk, legs, ears, and tail, I thought about how to get my father out of trouble.

It seemed to me that if anybody was going to catch the arsonist, it wasn't going to be the police. They thought they'd already caught him. They also don't hang around town enough to find out anything. San Puerco doesn't have a police department. We're covered by the county sheriff, who, of course, is over the hill and far away. It takes them thirty minutes to get here in an emergency. So if there was going to be a detective working on this case, it would have to be me.

It seemed to me that the arsonist must be an enemy of Meyer Tate's since both of the burned buildings had belonged to him.

Now who could be an enemy of Meyer Tate?

Anybody who knew him, that's who.

How do you catch an arsonist who sneaks around at night?

Maybe he'd set another fire while my father was still in jail. Then they'd know my father was innocent. Otherwise, there wasn't a whole lot of hope of catching the guy unless he made a stupid mistake.

Or somebody turned him in.

Somebody who knew him. Somebody who was keeping quiet because the arsonist was his friend, or because he was scared.

Somebody who wanted to collect a big reward.

I worked my way down the tree, and Flake yowled and danced and zipped off into the woods, and we walked home. I made Flake stay at my house, and walked over to Pinecone Way. I passed Danny's house. I passed the lot above, where smoke was still smoldering from the ruins. I climbed to the top of the hill and over Meyer Tate's gate and knocked on his door.

Meyer Tate opened the door. He saw me, and oddly, for a moment he looked frightened. Then he relaxed. "What do you want?" he said.

"I want you to help my father."

"*Help* your father? Of all people!"

"He didn't do it."

"The sheriff seems to think otherwise."

"They don't know my father. Do you know my father?"

"Yes, as a matter of fact, I do."

His answer surprised me. "How?" I asked.

"I sold him your house. I built it. That is, I hired the men who built it. Didn't you know that? If there is any ugliness in a person, it will come out in the course of a real estate transaction. Believe me, I've seen it all. Your father struck me as an honorable and honest man. One of the few such men in this town."

"Do you believe that he's an arsonist?"

"The sheriff believes so."

"Do you, Mr. Tate?"

He stared at me hard. Fighting the impulse to look away, I stared right back. His eyes weren't nearly as strong as a hawk's. In a moment, he looked away. He scratched the back of his neck. "No," he said. "I rather doubt it."

"Do you think he should be in jail?"

"I see no profit in that."

"Would you help me catch the real arsonist?"

Tate looked surprised. "Do you have any idea who it might be?"

"Somebody who hates you."

"I'm afraid that doesn't narrow the field very far."

"My father doesn't hate you."

"That's true. And that's to his credit."

"Would you offer a reward? Maybe if it's big enough, somebody will come forward with some information or maybe even know who it is."

Tate's eyes grew wide. "A reward? You mean *money*?"

"Maybe like ten thousand dollars."

"Ten thousand dollars?"

He clutched his chest. For a moment I thought he was having a heart attack, but it was only a gesture.

"Five thousand?" I said.

His lips were clamped tight.

"Five hundred?"

"Go away," he said. "Just please, go away."

"Your own house might be next, you know."

"I doubt that."

"You might even get burned up yourself. You might *die*."

"No, no."

"Why not?"

"Hmp. Well. I see your logic. My house does seem a likely target."

"Doesn't that worry you?"

"Of course. Of course. But . . . *ten thousand dollars*?"

"One thousand?" I said.

Tate snorted.

"One hundred?"

"Do you know the value of money?" Tate said.

"I have fifty-three dollars," I said. "I'm saving for a dirt bike. Listen. If you'll offer a reward, I'll put in the fifty-three dollars."

He looked confused. He stared at me. But he said nothing.

"So the answer's no?" I said.

Still he didn't answer.

"I'm sorry I bothered you," I said. "Maybe I can get some other people to offer a reward." Though I didn't have much hope of it. "Maybe everybody in town will chip in."

"Wait."

I waited.

Tate pulled on his ear. "Are you going to talk this up all over town?"

"Well, sure. How else can I get — "

"Wait. If you talk this up, will you tell people that you asked me first?"

"Well, sure. Because otherwise they'll just say, 'Ask Meyer Tate for a reward. After all, it's his buildings that are burning down.' "

"And if they find out that I refused to offer a reward, they'll think I — What will they think?"

"They'll just think you're a cheapskate."

Tate frowned.

"I mean," I said, "I'm just saying what they'll think."

Tate continued to pull on his ear. "I could say that I don't want to offer a reward because the arsonist has already been caught."

"That would be a lie, Mr. Tate. Don't ask *me* to lie for you. You already told me, and I'll say, because I think it's important, that you don't believe my father was the one who — "

"All right. Shut up." Tate put his hand to his eyes. "I really do care what the people of this town think of me. It matters for business." With his fingers he pulled his eyelids shut, then flipped them open. "Why is it that whenever you come to my door, it ends up costing me ten thousand dollars?"

"Then you'll do it?"

He didn't answer.

I waited.

He had his hand on his forehead as if he had a headache.

"Yes," Tate said at last. "I'll call the sheriff and offer a ten-thousand-dollar reward."

"That's very generous of you, Mr. Tate."

"Just good business," he said. Then he looked at me shrewdly. "That is, I'll offer nine thousand nine hundred and forty-seven dollars. Your fifty-three will make it even."

Ouch. Bye-bye, dirt bike. Somehow, I felt that I'd

been snookered. But I'd made the offer.

"All right," I said. "I'll get it now."

"Fine. As soon as I get it, I'll call the sheriff."

I ran straight home. I ran by the lake so fast, the goose didn't even have time to swim to shore but could only honk at me from the water. I had to walk the hill back up to Meyer Tate's.

I stood at his front door, heaving for breath. "Here's the money," I said. "There's fifty-two dollars and ninety cents. That's all I could find."

Tate dropped the money into his pocket. "You can owe me the dime," he said.

I turned to go. Then I stopped. I said, "Mr. Tate? Do you have another house where Danny can live?"

Tate raised his eyebrows. "Danny? Oh. *Them*. No. I have no place for *them*."

"Do you have to tear it down?"

"I'm improving the town, son. That shack is an eyesore. It's right across from the lake. That's prime property. I'm going to put up a nice new house — like yours. And then a better class of people will move into it. In a few years, all these old tumbledown shacks around town will be gone — and so will the people who live in them. This town will be a better place to live."

Somehow, the idea of San Puerco full of tidy new houses didn't fill my heart with joy. In fact, it made me sick to my stomach. All those cranks and dreamers who my dad was so fond of — like Patrick searching

for his comet — and all those poets who my mom
was always meeting with, and all those people like
Danny and his father who couldn't afford anything
better — where would they go?

I realized as I left Tate's house that I hadn't once
gotten tongue-tied while talking to him. He didn't
scare me any more. In fact, he seemed to grow smaller
each time I saw him.

Walking down the hill, I came to Danny's house
and turned into his yard. The screen door was hanging
by one hinge. I opened it, and it hung at an angle. I
knocked, and flecks of paint fell from my knuckles.
Inside I could see the big new television set and beside
it, on orange crates, the new stereo system.

Danny's father came to the door. He saw me and
his eyes narrowed. "You!" he said. "What's your old
man gonna burn down next?"

I didn't want to run away.

I didn't want to cry.

What I felt, and more and more as each moment
passed, was angry.

"Well," said Danny's father, "what do you say?"

"He didn't do it," I said. "Did you?"

"Me? Of course not." He looked surprised.

"Do you like Meyer Tate?"

"Me? He's *evicting* me."

"Somebody seems to want to burn down all of
Meyer Tate's properties. Somebody who hates him."

"Hmm." Danny's father chewed on his lip. "Well,

it ain't me. But you may be right. Now who'd want to do that to old Miser Tate?" He snickered. "Who *wouldn't*?"

"There's a ten-thousand-dollar reward for information about the arsonist."

"Who put up the money?"

"Tate."

"Tate? Well, well. He must be worried that his own house will be the next to burn."

"Do you know anything? Did you hear or see anything last night?"

"Nope."

"Did Emma?"

"I haven't seen Emma since yesterday. She never came home last night."

"Is Danny home?"

His father shrugged. "How would I know?" He called over his shoulder: "Hey, Danny boy!"

No answer.

So I walked up to Babcock's house.

12.
House Rules

Babcock lived in one of the new houses in town. Babcock and Danny were both in the driveway, taking turns on a yellow skateboard. Babcock had one of the few level driveways in all of San Puerco, so you'd think he could learn to be one of the best skateboarders in town.

He wasn't.

Babcock was terrible. As I watched, he wobbled along for about five feet, then crashed to the ground and rolled one way as the skateboard rolled the other.

He stood up, brushed his hands over his pants, and wiped his face with a blue handkerchief. Then he saw me.

"Hey Boone," he said, "is it true that your father's in jail?"

There are few secrets in San Puerco. I'd only found out a couple of hours ago myself, and yet by now everybody in town already knew about my father. I felt a slimy ball in the pit of my stomach, as if I'd eaten a wormy apple, but it wasn't food. It was anger.

It wasn't fair that my dad was in jail. It wasn't fair that I had to answer for it. It wasn't fair that somebody was burning down buildings, or that Danny was being evicted, or that the town — my Phobos — was going to turn into a new housing tract. *Nothing* seemed fair right now. Or, as my father would say:

It's the Banana Effect.

Just thinking of my dad's face, the wry smile as he explained those words, the wry smile he had for everything, at least everything when he wasn't angry, made me relax. He was still there. He might be in jail, but he was still with me in my mind. And as he once told me, the thing about the Banana Effect is, *good things will come in bunches, too*.

"What's it to you?" I said.

"Just wondering." Babcock shrugged. He walked over to fetch the yellow skateboard. "I mean, it's not every day that one of my friends has a father in jail. I thought it was kind of, um, *unusual*. Kind of *interesting*. That's all."

"Yes. But he didn't do it."

"Of course. I know."

"How do you know?"

"Because you said so."

"Thanks."

"Also because he'd have no reason to do it. Everybody knew he hated the Pub, so when he was caught out there with a can of gasoline, it did look kind of suspicious. But an empty house? What's the point?"

"The point is, somebody hates Meyer Tate. Hates him enough to burn down his buildings."

Danny broke in. "Everybody hates him," he said.

"Not so," Babcock said. "Not any more. He gave all that money to the soccer team. He could have weaseled out of it. But he did it. And people respect him for it. And they feel sorry for him what with all his buildings burning down."

"They're gonna respect him even more," I said. "He's offering a ten-thousand-dollar reward for information about the arsonist."

"Ten thousand smackers!" Danny slapped his forehead. "Is he eating loco weed?"

"Sounds like good business to me," Babcock said. "He probably figures, first of all, if the arsonist *is* Boone's father, then he won't have to pay the reward. And if it isn't, then ten thousand dollars is probably worth it if it keeps his own house from burning down."

"Whatever he does, I'm sure he'll make a profit," I said. "Meyer Tate would probably make a profit on his own funeral. And the way things are going, if Tate died, my father would probably be arrested for his murder. You know what I heard? He can claim the money he gave the soccer team as a business expense. It's a tax deduction."

"Of course," Babcock said, handing me the skateboard. "Also, it was good public relations for him. So is offering a reward. People in town are going to think of him as a good and generous man. And maybe he is, at that."

Danny nearly choked on that last idea. "Dsh," he finally managed to say, coughing. "Not if he evicts them."

Then Babcock said something that surprised me: "What can we do to help your father?"

"I dunno. Nothing." With a finger, I twirled a wheel on the skateboard that I was holding in my hand. "Find the arsonist, I guess."

Danny said, "Maybe we could picket the jail."

Babcock shook his head. "Wouldn't help," he said.

"Why not? It worked for soccer."

"This is different," Babcock said. "Now, how can we find the arsonist?"

I had no idea. But I felt better already. Just knowing that Babcock wanted to help — that I had friends on my side — gave me hope.

I took a turn on the skateboard. I wasn't much better than Babcock.

Then Danny took a turn. He's good. He turned a figure eight around Babcock and me, then skated toward Babcock's garage so fast I thought he'd crash, dragged to a sudden stop, stepped on the back end of

the board to flip it up into his hand — and missed.
Just barely missed. The skateboard slipped like a big
yellow banana peel right past his hand and up into
the air where Danny swiped at it with his other hand,
which instead of grasping it actually batted it further
along.

The skateboard flew away from Danny into the open
garage. It bounced off the hood of a car and clattered
to the floor.

Babcock trotted over and looked at the car. There
was a scuff mark on the white paint of the hood. It
was an old MG, the kind with the square front end,
and it was obviously well cared for. Somebody had
waxed it to a high shine — except for the gray streak
on the hood.

"Uh-oh," Babcock said.

"It wasn't *my* fault," Danny said.

"I suppose it's mine?" Babcock said.

"It's the *skateboard's* fault," Danny said. "It must
be *defective* or something."

"Tell it to my father," Babcock said, shaking his
head. "He really loves that car. He's out here buffing
and waxing it at least once a week."

Danny looked scared.

"He enters it in rallies," Babcock said. "Part of your
score is based on looks."

Danny glanced around quickly and said, "Is he
home right now?"

Babcock said, "He just walked down to the store."

Danny's eyes darted about — and lighted on a can of white spray paint. "Ah-ha!" he said.

"Wait," Babcock said.

Danny was already shaking the can.

"Danny," Babcock said, "I think you better talk to my — "

Psssst.

Babcock looked stunned. He looked at Danny as if Danny had just taken a sledgehammer and pounded it into the hood of the MG.

Danny smiled. "There," he said. "All fixed."

"I don't believe it," Babcock said softly.

"Believe it," Danny said. "I can fix anything."

"Fixed? Look at it. Look at the edge. You can see where you sprayed and where you didn't."

Danny bent over the hood, looking closely at the little patch of paint. "So?" he said. "I'll just feather it out."

"Danny — "

Psssssssssssssssssssst.

Babcock staggered backward and leaned against the wall of the garage. He wiped his brow with a handkerchief. "It's worse," he said.

Danny wasn't smiling now. He looked worried. "I'll fix it," he said.

Psssssssssssssssssssst.

The circle grew wider.

Psssssssssssssssssssst.

"Danny. Stop."

Psssssssssssssssssssst.

Danny was looking mighty nervous. No matter how wide a circle he sprayed, you could still see the edge.

"Danny, I really don't think — "

"Shut up."

Pssssssssss-sp-sp-sp.

With a sputter, he was out of paint. He'd covered practically the entire hood.

"Gimme your hanky," Danny said, and he wiped Babcock's blue handkerchief over some dots on the lower part of the windshield. The paint smeared over the glass. "Quick," Danny said. "Where's some paint thinner?"

Babcock crossed his arms. "I'll never tell," he said.

But Danny was operating at about five times the speed of Babcock. He zipped like a dragonfly to some shelves in the back of the garage and came back with a can of paint thinner. He was moving so fast, I could hardly follow with my eyes. He poured some thinner onto the handkerchief and rubbed it on the glass until the smears had disappeared.

"There," Danny said with a nervous smile. "All fixed." He handed the handkerchief back to Babcock.

Babcock held the handkerchief in his palm and stared sadly at the white smears of paint on the cloth. Then, just as sadly, he stared at the car.

So did Danny. So did I.

The paint was sagging. There were drip marks, shiny spots, dull spots. And the color was a different white from the rest of the MG.

"Shut up," Danny said.

"I didn't say anything," Babcock said.

"Just shut up." Danny paced back and forth. Then he clapped his hands. "I got an idea!"

"I don't want to hear it."

"It's simple! We'll set it on fire! The car! We'll say the arsonist did it. Then he won't see what happened to the — "

"Danny!"

"Yeah. Right. Dsh. How do you set a car on fire, anyway?"

Danny looked like a cat surrounded by dogs.

"Don't worry," Babcock said. "My father won't kill you. That would be murder. He'll probably just beat the crap out of you."

"Not if I — "

"WHAT ARE YOU DOING?"

Danny's eyes had fastened on the dashboard of the car — and the key in the ignition. In a flash Danny had jumped into the driver's seat. He turned the key. He didn't have his foot on the clutch, and the car was in gear, so when he turned the key the entire car lurched forward.

Babcock leaped out of the way.

Danny stepped on the clutch. Then he turned the key again and actually got the engine started.

"NO!" Babcock shouted.

Danny let in the clutch — too fast — and the MG coughed forward out of the garage, then stalled. Again, Danny turned the key.

Babcock took two steps and jumped into the car

on top of Danny just as the motor came to life again. Danny's foot fell off the clutch as Babcock was squashing him into the seat, and the car lunged sideways across the driveway. Babcock grabbed the steering wheel and turned it just in time to avoid a tree, and at the same moment the engine died or else Danny hit the brake, but anyway, the car jerked to a stop and Babcock fell off Danny and standing there, right in front of the car, was Babcock's father with a pipe in his mouth and a small bag of groceries in his hands.

The pipe fell out of his mouth.

Babcock fell out of the car.

Danny took one moment to size up the situation and then leaped out of the MG. He hit the ground running. In five seconds he was gone.

Babcock's father — Mr. Babcock — stared after Danny. Then he picked up his pipe. Then he set the bag of groceries on the hood of the car — and saw the new paint.

Babcock was still lying on the driveway where he'd fallen. His eyeglasses lay several feet away. He made no move to stand up or to reach for the glasses.

"Are you hurt, son?" Mr. Babcock asked.

"No, sir."

"Wouldn't you like to stand up?"

"No, sir. I'll just stay here. It'll save you the trouble of knocking me down."

Mr. Babcock nodded. "That's thoughtful of you, son. Now I can start right in on stomping you."

"Yes, sir."

Mr. Babcock lit his pipe. He picked up the eyeglasses and handed them to his son. Then he turned to me. Calmly, he asked, "So what happened?"

"I didn't do it," I said. And I wasn't going to tell on people, either.

"I didn't ask that. I asked what happened."

"The skateboard," I said. "It . . . sort of . . . flew."

Mr. Babcock smiled. "All by itself? It has wings like a bird?"

"Well . . . it was in the air, anyway, and it . . . you know."

"I don't know."

"It scuffed the hood."

"Oh really? All by itself?"

"And so then the paint was to try to fix it. Only the edge showed, so the paint got bigger and bigger, but the edge kept showing."

"The paint," Mr. Babcock nodded. "All by itself." He chuckled. "Untouched by human hands."

"But then the paint ran out, and the paint thinner on the rag was for getting some spots off the windshield."

"The paint thinner. The rag." Mr. Babcock was laughing now. "They just jumped off the shelf. Right?"

"It wasn't a rag," Babcock said, getting to his feet. "It was my handkerchief. *Was*. Now it's a rag."

"Your handkerchief." Mr. Babcock slapped his knee, laughing hard.

"So then the key was in the ignition, so — "

"The key."

" — so I think the plan was to drive the car somewhere and hide it or maybe fix it and bring it back
or maybe — maybe . . ."

Mr. Babcock was laughing so hard, he had to lean
against the front of the car — which put a circle of
white paint on his blue jeans. And where his pants
had rubbed on the hood, I saw the original paint of
the car and the gleam of the wax.

When he was finished laughing, he said, "Now I've
heard all about a skateboard, and paint, and keys, and
all these *things*. But I haven't heard the most important words of all. I haven't heard anybody say, *'We
did it.'* And then somebody could say, *'We're sorry.'* "

It wasn't *we*, I wanted to say. It was Danny. But
then I asked myself, what had I done to stop him?

"Mr. Babcock," I said. "I'm sorry."

He smiled. "That's all right," he said. "Now, it looks
like you boys have a job to do."

"Boys?" Babcock said. "Boy *zuh*? It seems to me,
only one boy has a job to do."

"House rules," Mr. Babcock said. "You know that,
son. It's the responsibility of you and your friend here.
And, of course, your other friend who ran away."

"What job, sir?"

"Buff the car. There's so much wax on it, the paint
won't stick. And the scuff mark that started all this.
I'll bet it buffs out, too. I'll show you how."

"Yes, sir."

"Now go find your friend. If he's still your friend."

Well, yes, he was still *my* friend, at least. Babcock was too disgusted to help me look, but I found Danny by myself the first place I searched — sitting by the lake, tossing pebbles.

"Danny," I said, "you're *dangerous*."

"I guess I blew it, huh?"

"Where'd you learn how to drive?"

"I don't know how to drive. I never done it before."

"What were you planning to do with the car?"

"Crash it. So he wouldn't notice the paint."

"Well, he noticed."

"What'd he say?"

"He wants you to come back and fix it."

"I'll bet he wants to fix *me*, too."

"No. He *laughed*. He's the calmest man I've ever seen. If it'd been my dad, he would've been *screaming*."

Danny shuddered. "Mine would've bounced my head like a basketball."

"Mr. Babcock says it'll buff off. The paint couldn't stick to the wax. And the scuff mark. It'll buff out, too. We're gonna help you."

"Why?"

"Mr. Babcock said we had to. House rules."

"House rules?"

"House rules."

"What's that mean?"

"It means, like, rules are different from one house to another."

"*That's* no lie."

"I kind of like Babcock's house rules."

"They mean you have to help me get out of my mess."

"I don't mind. I help you, someday you'll help me."

"Yeah. Right. House rules. Different. Dsh. And fathers," Danny said. "Fathers are different."

"And mothers," I said.

"Or whatever," Danny said.

"Meaning, what?"

"Meaning, don't call Emma my mother."

"So are you coming?"

Danny stood up. "How do you buff a car?"

"He'll show us."

"Dsh." Meaning, show me. Meaning, thanks for coming after me and sorry I ran away. Meaning, we're friends.

Danny was still sitting there on the dirt by the lake. The goose was swimming nearby, close enough to watch but far enough to be out of reach. He didn't trust Danny. He had good natural instincts.

"Come on," I said.

Danny looked up at me. He started to rise, then hesitated. I could see that something was puzzling him.

"What?" I said.

"Boone?"

"What?"

Danny scratched his ear. He said, "Dsh?"

Meaning, how do you figure out this world where one father would wallop you, another would shout, and another would *laugh*? Meaning, what are the house rules on this planet?

Dsh, I think, was one of the toughest questions I'd ever been asked.

13.
The Better Person

Monday morning I went to school, and my mother went to meet with our attorney. She said my father should be home for supper.

He wasn't.

They really thought he was the arsonist, and they were afraid that if they let him out on bail, he'd start another fire.

It was the quietest supper we'd ever had.

That night, I heard sirens.

The next morning, Tuesday, I learned that there'd been a fire in Meyer Tate's garage. Luckily for Tate, he'd seen it in time and managed to put it out himself with an extinguisher and a garden hose.

And, of course, it was lucky for my father as well. Now they couldn't claim that keeping him in jail was preventing fires. He had an ironclad alibi, literally, that he hadn't set fire to Meyer Tate's garage.

That evening, my father came home for supper.

It was a noisy, happy supper. I think I was happiest of all. I felt that I'd been let out of a jail of my own. I could go back to being a kid.

My dad hadn't shaved, but unlike last time when he'd come home from jail looking beaten and broken down, he was in a great mood. "I think I'll grow a beard," he said. "This is just like the Sixties."

"What Sixties?" I said.

"The nineteen sixties," he said. "The decade. When I went to college and had a beard and went to jail. Twice."

"You did! What for? Arson?"

My father laughed. "Arson? Of course not."

"What, then?"

"Once, for putting a daffodil in a policeman's pocket."

"That's a crime?"

"In the Sixties it was, yes."

"What was the other?"

"The other time, for pouring a cup of blood on a woman's desk."

"What did you do that for?"

"For protesting the draft. The war."

"What war?"

My father looked at me curiously. "The Vietnam War. The one Danny's father was in."

"You broke the law?"

"Well. The war was against the law. I was just trying to call people's attention to that."

"But . . . then . . . what about Danny's father? Was he breaking the law because he was fighting in the war?"

"No, no. He had to fight."

"But . . . then . . . why didn't *you* have to fight?"

"Because I was in school. Because I had a high lottery number. Because I was very, very lucky. And Danny's father was very, very unlucky. He did the right thing to fight. And I did the right thing, too, because I was trying to bring him home so he wouldn't have to fight anymore."

"Huh?" I said.

My father was shaking his head. "Isn't it amazing?" he said. "The government held a lottery. Nowadays, if you win a lottery, they give you money. Back then, if you lost the lottery, they sent you across the ocean with a gun and a prayer."

"This is . . . confusing," I said.

"It was confusing back then, too," my father said, and he rubbed his fingers over the stubble on his cheeks.

My mother asked me to go out to the garage and get some apple cider she'd been storing there. As I walked by the workbench, I happened to look underneath — and I noticed that the crossbow was missing. I hadn't moved it since the day I'd thrown it under the workbench after Danny had tried to shoot the goose.

Walking over to Danny's house, I saw signs stapled onto every telephone pole:

REWARD
$10,000
FOR INFORMATION LEADING TO THE ARREST OR CON-
VICTION OF THE ARSONIST RESPONSIBLE FOR BURNING
PUERCO PUB OR HOUSE OR GARAGE ON PINECONE
WAY. CONTACT COUNTY SHERIFF.
REWARD OFFERED AS A PUBLIC SERVICE BY
MEYER TATE

I saw a woman reading one of the signs and nodding her head in approval. Babcock was right. Meyer Tate knew how to use public relations to his advantage.

Flake was walking with me. At the duck pond, Flake suddenly stopped. The fur stood up on the back of his neck. He growled.

Damon Goodey was sitting on a boulder.

Even the dragonflies stayed away from him.

"Come on, Flake," I said.

Flake yowled.

Goodey scowled.

I pulled Flake by the neck and he started trotting alongside me, still yowling.

"You better shut that dog up," Goodey shouted. "Hey! How does your father like being in jail? He got no right to call the sheriff on me. I never been in jail. Now who's the better person? Huh? Who's the better person?"

No contest, I thought, but I didn't say anything.

When I got to Danny's house I went to the door, and Flake disappeared.

I knocked. Danny came to the door. I said, "The crossbow's missing."

"Oh?"

"I left it under the workbench in the garage, and now it's gone."

I was waiting for Danny to react, but again all he said was, "Oh."

"Do you happen to know anything about it?"

"Um. Sort of."

Just then, I heard a splash.

I looked at Danny. Danny looked at me.

The sound had come from somewhere outside and near by.

Danny walked around one side of the house while I walked around the other. We met in back where there was a fifty-five-gallon oil drum with the lid cut off, standing upright, full of scummy water. And in the water with his head sticking out and two paws over the rim was Flake, looking pleased with himself.

I said, "What's the matter, Flake? You hot?"

Danny said, "I guess he's a water dog."

Flake pulled himself up onto the edge of the barrel and jumped down at our feet. Standing between me and Danny, he gave himself a mighty shake — and sent us running for cover.

When we regrouped, I said, "Did you take the crossbow?"

"Sort of."

"Where is it?"

"It's half mine, you know."

"Maybe. But it's also half mine."

"So it's my turn to keep it."

"You gonna shoot things with it?"

"I might."

"No goose, Danny."

"Okay."

"Just targets, Danny."

"Okay."

"No living things, Danny."

"Okay."

"Promise?"

"Dsh."

And, solemnly, we shook hands.

With a roar, Walt stopped his motorcycle in front of Danny's house. Flake ran up and barked at him as if this were his house and he was going to protect it.

Walt said, "Is Emma home?"

Danny shook his head.

Walt took a brochure out of his pocket and waved it at us. "Australia!" he shouted. Then he kickstarted the Harley, goosed the gas a couple of times, and drove away.

Walking home, I saw Damon Goodey still sitting on his boulder next to the lake. I doubled back to avoid him — and encountered Patrick standing in front of a telephone pole with a handful of mail. He was reading the reward poster. He was wearing his usual red suspenders. He was oval-shaped, so I guess a belt wouldn't have anything it could grip.

"My, my," he said as I passed by. "That's quite a sum of money."

"I hope somebody gets it," I said. "I hope they catch that guy."

"So do I. So does your father."

"My dad's okay. They let him come home."

"On bail."

"He's free."

"But they didn't drop the charges."

"They didn't?"

"Didn't he tell you that? He's still got a trial date. Maybe he didn't want to worry you. I shouldn't have spoken. I'm sorry. That's old Patrick. Always running off at the mouth."

Patrick looked worried. I guess he could see the effect his words were having on me. Like a ball and chain.

So it still wasn't over. My father was still in danger. If he went out walking at night, and there was another fire . . .

"Patrick?"

"Yes?"

"Would you do me a favor? Would you tell my father not to come to your observatory anymore? Until they catch the guy? It seems like every time he goes out at night, he gets blamed for another fire."

Patrick hooked his thumbs under his suspenders

and said, "I can't tell Tom what to do."

"Could you *ask* him?"

"I could advise him, I suppose. Do you think somebody's out to get Tom?"

Until that moment, it hadn't occurred to me. But maybe so. Maybe it wasn't an enemy of Meyer Tate's. Maybe it was an enemy of my father's.

Damon Goodey.

Click.

All the circuits snapped shut in my brain.

Damon Goodey.

Of course.

Patrick was still talking. "Nobody's out to get your father," he was saying. "I've known Tom a long time. A *long* time. Believe me, he just doesn't make enemies. Why, I remember we were stoned one time, and this feller came up to your father and — "

"What? Stoned?"

"Did I say stoned?" Patrick looked embarrassed.

"You said stoned."

"Yes, well, never mind that, the point is, one time he — "

"That's a lie!" I said.

"What is?"

"My father would never get stoned."

Patrick looked at me sadly. "That's old Patrick," he said. "Always running off at the mouth."

"He *hates* drugs."

"Did Tom tell you he never took drugs?"

"He told me never to take drugs."

"Not you. Him. Did he tell you that he never took a drug in his life?"

"Not exactly. No. But he — "

"We were hippies, you know."

"You were?"

"I think it's time for old Patrick to take his mouth back home. Good-bye, Boone."

When I heard the Volkswagen bus pull to a stop on the street outside our house (you couldn't mistake that sound), I ran out and caught my father before he could get out of his seat. He was wearing a suit and tie. He'd just picked up his briefcase and was opening the door on the driver's side.

"Were you a hippie?" I asked.

My father set the briefcase on the steering wheel. "Come here," he said, and motioned for me to go around to the other side of the bus.

I took the seat up front on the passenger's side.

"I don't know what a hippie was," he said, leaning forward onto his briefcase. "That's just a name."

"Did you take drugs?"

My father grimaced. I saw his whole body tense. But he didn't answer.

"Did you?" I asked again.

"I knew some day I'd have to answer this question from my children," he said.

"Did you take drugs?"

"I smoked marijuana."

"Once? Twice?"

My father squirmed. He said, "Quite often, as a matter of fact."

I didn't know what to say. I stared at this man with scuzzy beard stubble on his face who I thought I had known. Finally, I asked, "What about other drugs?"

"No. I didn't. Most of my friends did, but I didn't. Not because I didn't approve of them, exactly, but because I was scared of them. I saw what sometimes happened."

He looked at me for a reaction.

I don't know how I looked, but I know how I felt: confused. Frightened. And pleased, to my surprise, happy, somehow, to know that my father was confiding in me.

My father said, "I enjoyed marijuana. Then I stopped after a while because it made me so fuzzy-headed."

If you asked me, I'd say my father was *still* fuzzy-headed. Absentminded, at least. I wondered if he was born that way or if the marijuana had made him that way for the rest of his life.

"I won't apologize for what I did," my father said. "And I won't for what the others did, either. At the time it seemed right. We didn't know as much about drugs and these things as we do now. Now we know about *addiction*. About *body* damage. *Brain* damage. We know some drugs are much worse than others. We have new drugs, now, that weren't even *invented* back then. A lot of things have changed. A whole lot of things. But marijuana? Is it any worse than alcohol?"

"Dad! Alcohol is poison! If something is only as bad as alcohol, that's pretty bad."

"You're right. That's a good point."

"Are you ever going to smoke it again?"

"I haven't for twenty years."

"But will you smoke it again sometime?"

"I don't want to right now."

"But will you want to again sometime?"

"It's illegal. I don't break laws any more. I'm a father. I have to set a good example."

"What if your friend had some? What if Patrick was smoking it?"

"That would be his business." My father was staring out the windshield.

"What if I told you I have some marijuana?"

"FOR GOD'S SAKE, DON'T SMOKE IT!" He practically leaped over the steering wheel.

My ears rattled.

"Do you really have some?" he said.

"No," I said. "I just wanted a reaction."

"I guess I gave you one." He shook his head. "Marijuana can damage a growing body. Let your cells grow without any drugs in them."

"But later?" I said. "When I'm grown? You think it's all right?"

"No, I didn't say that. But when you're grown, you won't be listening to me, anyway. You'll make up your own mind. You're old enough now to learn that most issues aren't black and white. When kids are young — Clover's age, or Dale's — we try to keep it simple. But you're old enough to learn more, now. And you're old enough that I can't control everything you do, anyway. Tobacco, alcohol, marijuana . . . even sugar. And caffeine. There're lots of nasty temptations in the world. And they all wreck your body. Is the pleasure worth the damage? Probably not. But I can't watch over you every second. You'll have to make up your own mind on how you should handle these things when you grow up. I'll advise you. But I can't control you. I don't know, Boone. What do you think you should do about these things?"

I had no desire to try marijuana, or alcohol, or tobacco, or caffeine. But I like sugar. Is it really a poison, too?

I'd wanted an answer, and he'd given me new questions. It seemed that the more I learned from my father, the less I knew.

Danny and I rode to the next soccer game and back in Jack Bean's truck. We won. Geraldine pulled a hat trick — scored three goals. Afterward, Walt gave her a hug. Then Dylan tried to give her a hug, but she sidestepped it and tripped him by using an aikido move that sent him sprawling on the grass.

Jack dropped Danny and me both off at Danny's house.

A moment later, Walt pulled up on his motorcycle. "Where's Emma?" he asked. "She inside?"

Danny shrugged. We walked to the house, to the screen door hanging on one hinge. "Wait here," he said, and he went inside alone.

He came back out with his father.

"Is Emma home?" Walt said. "I've been trying to talk to her for days now. There's a discount fare I can get for Australia if we pay in advance. We collected enough, with this discount, to pay for all of our tickets."

"So you need the money now?" Danny's father said. He looked down at the rotten floorboards of the porch.

"Today's the last day for the discount," Walt said.

Danny's father looked up at Walt. "Emma's gone," he said. "All gone, I reckon."

"Did you — and her — did you — "

"No," Danny's father said. He suddenly looked very tired. "She just said she was going out to buy some hanging ferns. She thinks all the classy houses have hanging ferns. That was a week ago. She didn't pack or nothin'. She just didn't come back."

"Where's the bank book?" Walt asked.

We walked into the house, which had a smell like fermenting orange peels. There were peanut shells on the floor next to a recliner chair with stuffing bursting out of the armrest.

"It's probably in here," Danny's father said, pointing to a room containing a double bed, a dresser, and mounds of clothing everywhere. The smell in there was like the water that's left in a vase after the flowers have died.

Danny's father started opening drawers in the dresser. Walt picked up clothes from on top of the bed, shook them, and tossed them aside. Danny crawled under the bed and came back out covered with dust, dragging a suitcase. He flipped the catches: *sproing, sproing.*

Inside, on top, was a white dress. Walt lifted it out and held it up. It was a fancy piece of clothing with ruffles and little embroidered roses, and on one side near the top was a pin with some ribbon and something that looked like a dead vegetable with a brown stain on the fabric underneath.

"A corsage," Walt whispered. Then he set the dress gently aside.

Danny was searching through the pockets of the suitcase.

"Nada," he said.

Danny's father was looking through the wastebasket. He pulled out a small blue bank book with a travel brochure tucked between the pages. He flipped it open. His eyes bulged. He looked as if he'd been slapped in the face with a wet salmon. He closed the bankbook and handed it to Walt.

Walt flipped it open. He sucked in his breath. He blew it out slowly, like the last air being squeezed out of an inner tube. He said, "It looks like all our Trashathon paid for was a television set. And a stereo. And a Caribbean cruise."

I felt as if I'd been kicked in the chest.

Walt rushed to the telephone in the other room. I could hear him clicking buttons. And I knew he was too late.

Emma had stolen all the money from the Trash-athon. She'd stolen from a bunch of *kids*.

"Danny," I said, "you win."

"Win what?"

"The bet. I owe you one billion dollars."

And Danny gave me a look that said, sadly, welcome to the planet.

14.
A Furious Fossil

I took Danny to my tree. We didn't even change out of our soccer clothes, but as we walked by my house, I let Flake loose so he could come with us.

My father spotted me looking gloomy and asked, "What's the matter?"

"Nothing," I said.

"Baloney," he said.

For some reason that I didn't understand, I didn't want to tell him about Emma. I left my father standing with his hands on his hips, watching Danny and Flake and me walking up the street and into the forest. We climbed the branches wearing our soccer uniforms, cleats, and shinguards. The cleats were a help for climbing.

Flake lay down at the foot of the tree.

"Ga-a-a-a-awd!" Danny said. "This is amazing."

We sat on separate branches, two feet apart. Danny was higher.

"We could build a fort," Danny said. "Let's come back tomorrow with boards and nails and stuff. Let's bring Babcock, too."

Clouds were blowing in off the ocean, swirling, changing shape as we watched. We could see their shadows rolling across the town and the hills and the forest. We could see Jack Bean's truck parked down by the duck pond.

"Mr. Babcock's waxing that MG again," Danny said, shading his eyes with his hand.

I was wondering why I hadn't wanted to tell my father about Emma. Suddenly I knew, and it was a terrible thought: *Maybe my father was lying.* Like Emma. Maybe he really did set those fires.

Could I trust him?

Can you trust any grown-up?

It was an awful moment.

I wished there were another old abandoned house we could wreck. I didn't care if it was wrong. I *wanted* to do something wrong.

In my mind, I smashed ten windows. *Smash smash smash smash. Smash smash. Smash smash smash. Smash.* I ripped a door off its hinges. *Cra-a-ack pop.* I kicked my foot through a wall. *Ka-thud.*

"Danny," I said, "did you know Emma was spending that money?"

"Dsh."

"Danny!"

"What?"

"What does that stupid *dsh* mean?"

"It means, I didn't know. But I should've."

So why was I yelling at Danny? He didn't steal the money. Neither did my father. Nobody was responsible for Emma — except Emma. And I even felt a little sorry for her. She'd get caught sooner or later. And even if she didn't, she'd have to live with herself, with knowing she was a thief. And I bet that Caribbean cruise wasn't as great as she expected.

As I looked out from the tree, I wondered, why go to the Caribbean? Who would want to be anywhere but here?

In my mind I repaired all the broken windows with putty and new glass. I screwed the door back on its hinges and plastered the holes in the wall. Then I swept up the mess and heaved all the debris into a great big Dumpster. When the dust had settled and the last shard of glass had tinkled to the bottom of the Dumpster in my brain, I still trusted my father. I have to trust people. Especially him. All people. Otherwise, how can the world work? But I guess you have to be careful, too. Play the game fair, but watch for cheaters.

One of my father's rules, which I guess makes it a house rule, is that he'll trust somebody completely until he finds out — just once — that the person has cheated him. And then he'll never trust that person again.

Or at least, that's the way he's always explained the rule to Clover and Dale and me.

It seems to me, though, even if you're going to trust somebody, you have to be at least a little cautious. And the less you know them, the more you're cautious. Or in the case of *certain* people, the *more* you know them, the more you're cautious. I guess it's another one of those issues that starts out black and white for little kids, and gets grayer as you get older.

No wonder old people turn gray.

Danny and I didn't say anything for a long time. We just sat there, gazing out over our little world from our two separate branches.

We stayed in the tree until the sun went down.

"Tomorrow, you bring Babcock," Danny said. "I'll bring some boards."

The next morning, Sunday, I slept late. I'd been trying to sleep lightly so that I could hear if my father got up in the middle of the night to go out for a walk. I was planning to try to stop him. Tackle him, if I had to. But he never got up. When dawn came, I felt safe and dropped into a deep dream.

When I woke up, I was late. I skipped breakfast. I ran to Babcock's house and found him sitting cross-legged in his driveway, pounding a hammer on a large white rock. Little white chips flew off with each blow.

"What are you doing?" I asked.

"Finding fossils," he said without even looking up. He continued to chip away at the rock, which was the shape and size of a football.

"Found anything?"

"Trilobite."

"Is that a *dinosaur*?"

He looked up then. He set down the hammer and pushed his glasses back up on his nose. "Don't you know *anything*?" he said.

I knew that my planet was growing larger. And colder. But these were not scientific observations — in fact, science would say the opposite — so I didn't say anything.

"Trilobites used to rule the world," Babcock said. "Before dinosaurs. They lived underwater. They looked like this." He handed the big rock containing the little trilobite up to me.

The trilobite was about the shape and size of a walnut — with eyes. "How old is it?" I asked, turning the stone in my hands.

"About half a billion years."

Thud.

That rock dropped out of my hands as if it suddenly weighed a thousand pounds.

"Hey!" Babcock reached over and cradled the rock in his fingers, checking the fossil. "You could've *wrecked* it."

Which was exactly why my hands had dropped it, I think. They knew that they had no business holding something that had lived half a billion years ago.

Sometimes my hands seem to act on their own without any direction from my brain.

"Did I hurt it?" I said.

"You can't make it *hurt*," Babcock said.

"I know. I meant — "

"It can't *feel* anything. It's *dead*."

But Babcock was wrong. Just as my hands can sometimes move without thinking, so too my mind can sometimes know things without being taught. It was like seeing a ghost or receiving a message by mental telepathy. In this case, I knew something that defied science: Mr. Trilobite was *angry*. That fossil, that dead piece of stone which had laid in peace for half a billion years, it — or at least its spirit — was *furious* at Babcock for pounding on its bed with a hammer, and at me for dropping it onto an asphalt driveway — asphalt made of oil that was made from the decomposed swamp where that trilobite used to live.

Half a billion years. All that time there was a natural order to this planet — the slow building of continents, the ebb and flow of the sea, the gradual growth of new life — and then man comes along, and in a few quick years, we mess the whole place up. It's enough to make any fossil fighting mad.

But I said none of this to Babcock or I would've sounded like a fool. My mouth, like my hands, doesn't always connect perfectly with my brain. There are certain thoughts that I know I can't put into sounds or they'll come out the way I talked to Meyer Tate about the Trashathon — like garbage.

What I did say was, "My father says there were redwood trees during the Age of Dinosaurs. He says they're one of the oldest forms of life still existing today."

Babcock nodded. "And dragonflies," he said. "Back then, there were dragonflies the size of a *hawk*."

"Were there redwood trees when there were trilobites?" I asked.

Babcock shrugged.

Ah-ha! Something he didn't know.

"I found a tree," I said.

"Oh really?" Babcock smiled.

"I mean I found a tree we can climb way up in. You can see for *miles*. Danny and I are gonna build a fort. You wanna see?"

"Um. Okay." He didn't sound enthusiastic.

"Bring the trilobite. To show Danny. You have any boards?"

We gathered a few boards at Babcock's, a few at my house, plus a hammer and nails and a handsaw. Babcock carried the tools plus the trilobite rock, and I carried three boards. We'd need to come back for the rest. The boards were awkward — and heavy. Around my neck I'd strapped my father's binoculars.

Flake bounded ahead of us on the trail. I was sure he could pick up Danny's scent. When we got there, Danny was sitting on a root sticking out from a bank of the creek where it drops into the little pool, not far from the big tree. Danny was scratching Flake's one upright ear. Flake was sitting, wagging his tail, and cocking his head to the side so Danny could get a better reach at the ear. After me, Flake liked Danny more than anybody.

On the ground next to Danny lay two boards. "What's this?" he said, pointing to the rock in Babcock's hands.

"Fossil," Babcock said.

"It's a trilobite," I said. "They used to rule the world. It's half a billion years old!"

"Oh," Danny said. He wasn't interested. To him it was a dead rock.

Which to my mind made the trilobite even angrier. It couldn't get any respect.

"Where's the tree?" Babcock asked.

We walked over to its base. Babcock stood, looking up. After a few moments he said, "How will you get the boards up there?"

I looked at Danny. Danny looked at me.

"Don't you need both hands for climbing?"

We nodded.

"You need a rope," Babcock said. "Anybody bring a rope?"

We shook our heads.

"My dad's got one," Babcock said. "I'll go get it."

"Wait," Danny said. "Don't you want to climb the tree first? It's *awesome* up there."

Babcock looked up again, slowly.

"No," he said. "I'll go get the rope. Here. Take this." He handed me the stone. And he walked back down the trail.

Danny said, "You think maybe he's scared?"

I said, "I think he may be worried that he can't climb it."

"If he can't, let's tie the rope around his waist and *pull* him up."

"I think he can do it. I think Babcock can do just about anything he sets his mind to."

"You ready to go up?"

We climbed. I tucked the trilobite rock into my shirt, sort of wedging it under my belt.

It was an overcast day, threatening to rain. The air smelled damp and fresh with life. The quarry was silent, shut down for Sunday. A hawk circled lazily in the distance. A couple of men were shuffling around in the prison yard behind the chainlink fence.

I took the rock out of my shirt and held it in my hands. See, trilobite? I wanted to say. See how the world has changed? Roads and prisons and quarries — and the skeleton of another new house a-building. But we still have redwoods and dragonflies, just like the Age of Dinosaurs. You might feel at home in our pond — but watch out for the goose. You go over the hill to Pulgas Park, little trilobite, and you won't believe your eyes.

Danny said, "Why'd you bring that stupid rock all the way up here?"

"He's a friend," I said. "I'm showing him around."

"He's a *rock*. He can't *see*. He can't under*stand*."

"Yes," I said. "Sometimes I have that problem with my friends."

"Hey. We all got our problems."

I looked down at Flake lying in the duff at the foot of the tree with his head erect, alert, one ear cocked. I looked at the ranch on the hills across the valley, still brown. Soon the winter rains would turn them green for the cows. How many hundreds of years, I wondered, had this tree watched those hills change from green to brown to green again. Way down the valley I could see a flower farm — a square of white, another of red, another of yellow.

For a long time, we sat, doing nothing.

I was watching the lake. With my binoculars in one hand I could see the goose strutting along the shoreline like the emperor of the pond. I saw Babcock coming back with a rope looped over his shoulder. On the highway I saw a few cars, not like a normal Sunday, fewer, I guess, because people didn't want to go to the beach when it might rain.

And then I saw Damon Goodey. He was walking up the forest trail toward our tree.

I thought, just to be safe, I'd better go down and grab Flake before Goodey arrived.

I started down the tree.

Flake yowled. He leaped up against the base of the tree. Then he ran a big circle around the tree and shot off into the forest. And stopped when he saw Damon Goodey.

I was still only a third of the way down.

Flake growled. He bared his fangs.

Goodey bent down and picked up a rock.

Flake growled again.

Goodey wound up and threw the rock. It streaked through the air so fast, it was only a blur. It hit Flake on the front leg.

Flake yowled with pain and fell to the ground.

Goodey picked up another rock.

"Hey!" I shouted. "Don't hurt him."

Goodey looked around. He couldn't figure out where the voice was coming from. He jiggled the rock in his hand.

I shouted, "You leave my dog alone!" I moved down another branch. Flake was whimpering. He needed help.

Goodey looked up and spotted me. He couldn't see Danny, who was way up higher and hidden behind the trunk of the tree.

Goodey didn't say a word. He walked a little closer, scowling all the way. He wound up — and threw the rock. At me.

It struck a branch just below me making a sound like a hammer.

Without a word, Goodey picked up another rock. He reared back and fired. Missed. Then again. And again.

He had an arm, all right. Rocks were flying all around me. Goodey was in a frenzy. There was an endless supply on the shore of the creek. Stones whistled through the air. Sometimes they were deflected by lower branches. Sometimes they made it through. Sometimes I had to dodge. There's a limit to how much you can dodge when you're balanced on a branch way up above the ground.

I looked at Danny. He looked scared — scared for me. I didn't blame him for not showing himself. It would only get him stoned. I could try moving to another branch to put the trunk between myself and Goodey — but then Goodey would simply move to where he could see me, and then he'd spot Danny, too, which would only give him two targets instead of one.

The look in Goodey's eyes was totally wild, like a dog's in a fight.

Flake tried to stand up. He wobbled on three legs. The other one was bleeding. He collapsed and lay there in the duff, licking the wounded leg.

I wondered how long this could go on. Pretty soon, the law of averages guaranteed that he'd hit me, and it would hurt bad. It might even knock me out of the tree. I had to do *something*. The rocks were the size of golf balls . . . or trilobites.

I still had the trilobite rock in my hand. It weighed about ten pounds. I had the advantage of height. I didn't know if I could aim very well, but I'd have to trust my hands to do the right thing. I'd have to hit some piece of Goodey — somewhere that would hurt bad enough to make him quit. I hefted the rock a couple of times in my hand. With a rock of this size, from this height, any place I hit him would hurt bad. Very bad. I braced my feet on a branch and aimed straight at Damon Goodey's head, and told my brain to leave my hands alone and let them figure it out. The stone shook in my fingers and suddenly, without realizing it, I gave a heave and watched as the stone arched through the air. . . .

Thud.

Unfortunately, he saw it coming and stepped to the side.

The rock hit the ground and split in half.

Fortunately, one piece of the split bounced up and hit him on the thigh. Hit him hard.

Now Goodey looked even madder. He wound up to throw another rock — and grabbed the back of his head. Something else had hurt him. My trilobite rock? But it had hit him on the thigh. Ten seconds ago. Had it ricocheted back again?

Then again, Goodey grabbed his head, this time just above his ear. And then while he was still confused, he jerked again and slapped the back of his neck. I saw blood on the side of his head, and on his hand where he'd grabbed it. I saw something fly across the creek — like a fat dragonfly — and bounce off Goodey's skull.

He didn't know what was attacking him — or from where. He must have thought it was me.

With both hands in his hair, as if he had a massive headache, he started walking, then trotting, down the trail. I saw a rock fly after him and strike him in the back. He didn't turn around to look. He trotted faster, and in another five seconds, he was gone.

Out of the bushes, just on the other side of the creek from where Goodey had been standing, Babcock stepped forward with a rock in each hand. He'd been so close to Goodey, he almost could have tackled him.

Danny and I climbed down.

Flake's leg was a bloody mess. I pulled off my shirt and wrapped it around his leg. Then I picked him up in both my arms.

Babcock picked up the two halves of the stone that I'd thrown. Where it had fractured, a new trilobite was exposed.

Fortunately, it was all downhill to my house. I walked as fast as I could, but Flake was heavy. He bent his head up from my arms and licked me on the chin.

We didn't say a word until we were almost back to my street.

"Nice throwing," Danny said as we hurried along.

"Thanks," Babcock said.

Danny looked at him curiously. He said, "You know, you could've been hurt. If you'd missed."

"I know," Babcock said, panting. He wasn't used to walking this fast.

My arms ached under the weight of Flake.

"You could've got away," Danny said. "You didn't have to help us."

"Yes," Babcock said. "I did have to. House rules."

"House? What house?"

"Our house. The tree."

"Oh," Danny said, thinking it over. "Dsh," he said, liking the idea.

Together we walked out of the forest and onto my street.

15.
Life on Phobos

My dad rushed me and Flake to the vet. While we were driving, I told him about Emma stealing the soccer money and about Damon Goodey trying to stone Danny and me in the tree.

The vet said the rock had shattered a bone in Flake's leg. He'd live, but he'd always have a limp. He said Flake was in shock and should stay at the vet's overnight. "And you look a little pale yourself," he said to me.

I wasn't sure what it meant to be "in shock," but it sounded like the right words for the way I was feeling.

Back home, my father called the sheriff.

A half hour later, a sheriff's deputy appeared at our door.

I told him about Goodey throwing rocks.

"Did he hurt you?" the deputy asked.

"He hurt my dog."

"Did any *people* get hurt?"

"Just Goodey."

"I thought *he* was throwing at *you*."

"Yes, but we — that is, Babcock, mostly — hit him with some stones. I mean, Goodey started it."

"So you had a rock fight. And you won. And now you're complaining."

"He hurt my dog. He shattered his bone."

My father said, "The point is, Damon Goodey is wild. He's out of control. He's a danger to this community, especially to the children. Can't you do anything?"

I looked at my father standing beside me. Twice in the last month he'd been arrested, but he didn't seem at all frightened of the deputy. He was giving all his attention to me with a worried look on his brow.

The deputy said, "I'll talk to him. If I can find him. But I can't arrest him. There's nothing to charge him with."

The deputy had a kind but weary-looking face. He didn't look like the type of person who would arrest somebody for putting a daffodil in his pocket.

I guess times have changed.

Danny spent the night at my house. As we lay in the dark, Danny said, "What were you aiming at when you threw that rock out of the tree?"

"Damon Goodey," I said.

"What *part* of Goodey?"

"His head."

"You know what would've happened if a rock that size, from that high, hit Goodey on the head? You would've *debrained* him."

"Yeah," I said. "I guess."

"You made me promise not to ever shoot a living thing. With the crossbow. Then you went and tried to crack Damon Goodey's skull with a rock. You broke the rule." I heard him breathe in, then out, a sound like wind rustling in a tree. "You get to have all the fun," he said.

"If that was fun," I said, "I never want to have fun for the rest of my life."

"Hey, relax," Danny said. "Just putting you on."

To me, it was no joke; in fact, I suspected it wasn't to Danny, either. I don't like fighting. I don't like hurting people. But sometimes you have to defend yourself. I'd like to learn aikido. They say it's entirely defensive, a way to redirect the energy of an attacker so it goes back against himself.

I'd like to redirect all the bad energy of the world back against itself.

What would happen the next time Danny or I encountered Damon Goodey?

In the morning Danny and I were toasting bread in the kitchen when my little sister Clover came running out of the bathroom. She turned a somersault on the living room rug, then dashed into the kitchen and hugged the door of the refrigerator.

"What are you doing?" Danny said.

"Something I have to do," Clover said.

I was embarrassed. I knew what was coming. "Clover," I said, "please don't — "

"You see," she said, "after I flush the toilet I have to get out of the room, do a somersault, and then touch as many colors of paint as I can before the water does that gurgle thing — you know, when it goes down."

I expected Danny to laugh out loud.

Instead, Danny nodded seriously. "Oh. I see," he said. "I didn't know that one."

Clover said, "Do you know about tunnels? To hold your breath and stick up your finger?"

"Sure," Danny said. "Everybody knows that."

"You know about churches? And railroad tracks? And cemeteries? And if two people say the same word at the same time?"

"Of course," Danny said. "Do you know about 'flat'?"

"Flat?" Clover shook her head. "What's that?"

"If somebody burps, they have to say 'flat.' If they don't, somebody can say 'light switch,' and then they can hit him until he touches a light switch."

"Really?" Clover said. "I didn't know."

"You know 'Vince'?" Danny asked.

"Vince?"

"If I fart, I have to say 'Vince' before somebody else says 'doorknob,' or else they can hit me and keep hitting me until I touch a doorknob."

My father was laughing. He'd been sitting at the table, listening. "This sounds just like going to court," he said. "All these *rituals*."

"What's a ritular?" Clover said.

"Ritual. It's something that people started doing a long time ago, and nobody can remember why anymore, but they still feel that they have to do them or else something terrible might happen, although nobody knows just what it might be."

"And they do that in courtrooms?" Clover said.

"That's why people need lawyers," my father said. "They're the ritual guides. The navigators of ritual."

Clover nodded her head solemnly. "I see. You mean, in court, the lawyer tells you to say 'Vince.' Before the judge can say 'doorknob.' "

My father slapped his knee. "Exactly," he laughed. "Exactly that."

For the next week, Danny spent every night at my house. He said he didn't want to sleep alone, which was fine with me because I didn't want to, either. Also, as eviction day came closer, Danny's father became less pleasant to be around. Their phone had been disconnected. Walt had taken the new television and stereo set back to the store where Emma had bought them, but he couldn't get any money back because she'd only made a small down payment.

Danny liked staying at my house. He liked watching my dad work on the computer, and he liked playing games on it himself. He liked the fact that my mom fixed food for us instead of his having to fix it for himself. He liked the fact that nobody yelled at him, and he didn't seem to mind having to roll up his bedding every morning, and say "please" and "thank you" at the table, and be told when to go to bed. He liked having house rules — *any* rules, probably, would do.

One day, my father sent Danny and me to the store with a ten-dollar bill to buy some milk and peanut butter. As we passed Danny's house, Flake disappeared. We heard a splash. We continued to the store, where Danny took the change while I packed the bag. Flake wasn't waiting for us when we came out of the store. We remembered the splash.

When we'd walked back to Danny's, we looked in the barrel behind his house. There was Flake, pawing desperately with his one good front leg. He couldn't pull himself out. He might have drowned. When he was wet, both ears flopped down.

I grabbed him under the bad leg, pulled, and he hoisted himself out. Then he stood in front of Danny and me and shook scummy water all over our clothes.

It was one of those moments that made me wonder
why I ever wanted to have a dog.

Danny's father came out of the house. "Danny," he
said. "Pack your clothes."

"Why?" Danny said.

"I'm going to Oklahoma."

Danny's face clouded over. "I don't want to go to
Oklahoma."

"You got a better idea?"

"You go. Let me stay with Boone. At least for a
while." Danny looked at me. I nodded in approval.

"That okay with Boone's folks?"

We went home and asked my dad. He talked it over
with my mom. They said they didn't want to see Danny's schooling interrupted — which I didn't think was
a major worry of Danny's — and that they would be
happy to let him stay until his father found a new
place to settle down.

Meanwhile, I put the milk in the refrigerator and
the peanut butter on a shelf. My father said, "Where's
my change?"

Danny put some coins into my father's hand. Without even glancing at it, he dropped the money into
his pocket.

When he was gone, Danny whispered to me, "Does
he ever count the change?"

"Never," I said. "I guess those are house rules
around here. He says he'll trust you. He'll keep trust-
ing a person until he finds out — just once — that

he's been cheated, and then he'll never trust that person again. Ever."

Danny looked worried. He turned right around and left me. A half minute later, I heard him say to my father, "Uh, Mr. Barnaby? I forgot to give you this quarter."

16.
The Arsonist

Babcock found out that Danny was sleeping at my house, and asked if he could join us for the night before the next soccer game.

We said, sure.

Danny went back to his house for the first time in a couple of days so he could get his soccer uniform and cleats. Babcock and I went with him.

The house already looked abandoned. There were orange crates and the recliner chair with the stuffing coming out, and there was termite dust on the table and no food in the refrigerator . . .

. . . and empty bottles in the bathroom . . .

. . . and Damon Goodey's sleeping bag in the bedroom. We hadn't seen Goodey since the incident in the tree.

"He's sleeping *here*," Danny said. "In my *house*."

"It's not yours, now," Babcock said.

"It certainly isn't," Danny said. He gathered up all the rest of his clothes, and his soccer trophies, a pile of comic books, the crossbow, and a baseball card collection. It was everything he owned. We carried them back to my house.

We stayed up late eating popcorn and playing Dungeons and Dragons. We weren't going to be in very good shape for the soccer game. Then, after we'd finally gone to sleep, I felt Flake sit up beside me on the bed. I heard footsteps in the hallway outside my room.

I got up.

"What is it?" Babcock said from his sleeping bag on the floor.

"My father," I said. "I think he's going out."

Sure enough, I heard the back door open and close. Quickly, I pulled on pants and shoes.

"Where are you going?" Babcock asked.

"I'm going to follow him," I said.

"Can I come?" Babcock said.

"Hurry."

Babcock threw back the top of his sleeping bag, stood up, lost his balance in the dark, and stepped on Danny.

Danny woke up. "What are you doing?"

"Get dressed," Babcock said. "We're going to follow Boone's father."

"Where?"

"To the observatory, I hope," I said.

Neither Danny nor Babcock asked why I wanted to follow him in the dark of the night. Maybe they just thought it would be fun. Or maybe, like me, they were thinking of fires.

I knew my father wasn't setting fires. But I also knew that when he went out, fires seemed to happen. And I wanted to make sure they didn't happen tonight, or at least find out why they did.

I put a leash on Flake. I knew he'd try to catch up with my father. I wanted Flake to guide me, but I didn't want him to run up to my dad and give me away.

It was a perfect night for stars. No moon, and no fog. The Milky Way sparkled across the sky when you could see it through the trees. Flake tugged at the leash. We walked fast. Our breath made little clouds. There wasn't a sound in the whole town. Almost every window was dark.

I heard the goose honking down at the lake. At night, with no other noise to drown him out, you could probably hear him honking all over town. My father must have been walking past him.

We ran. We cut across a little meadow and through a clump of trees to stay away from the goose and from the streetlight that shines down by the lake. Jerking on the leash, Flake bounded at my side.

I could see my father up ahead as he passed near the light coming from somebody's porch. We slowed down. We passed Danny's house. Danny doubled back and ran to the side window and peeked inside. Then he ran and caught up with us.

"He in there?" I asked.

"Sleeping like the dead," Danny said. "Which I wish he was."

"Me, too," I said, but immediately it felt funny. It felt wrong to wish that somebody — even Damon Goodey — were dead. I just wished he were *gone*.

We climbed the hill.

Everything looked different at night. As we passed Meyer Tate's, where Patrick's driveway begins, I looked back and saw a view of the town as a collection of porchlights and streetlights. Not a car was moving. Not a person was stirring — at least, not where you could see them in one of the little pockets of light.

We started walking up Patrick's dirt driveway. It's a half mile to his observatory. He shares the driveway with about five other houses. It's full of ruts and bumps.

A little ways up, I heard the goose honking.

"Wait!" I said.

"What?" Babcock whispered.

"The goose. Somebody's down near the pond."

"So?"

"My father's going to be at the observatory for hours. I want to find out who's down by the lake."

"Me, too," Babcock said.

"You thinking what I'm thinking?" Danny said.

We ran down the hill. Downhill, Babcock can get

up a pretty good speed. I had trouble running and holding on to Flake at the same time, and finally my hand jerked one way as the leash jerked the other, and Flake was free.

We slowed down as we neared the bottom of the hill, then stopped before we got to Danny's house. Walking, we caught our breath. The goose had stopped honking. We tried not to make any noise. Flake was gone. I tried to listen for him, and heard a noise from behind Danny's house. Oh no, I thought, not the barrel.

I walked, still trying to be stealthy, around Danny's house and peeked around the corner.

I saw a man.

In the dark, he looked like a living shadow. He had a can of something, and he was splashing it on the side of Danny's house. I smelled gasoline. Just then, Flake appeared at my side from somewhere off in the bushes. He made a low growl in his throat, the kind of growl that you feel more than you hear.

The man was reaching for something in his pocket.

Flake left my side.

A spark. Then I saw a flame from a cigarette lighter.

Flake leaped against him. The man, the flame, and Flake all fell against the side of the house.

In an instant, there was a wall of flame. The house was on fire, and so was the man. His jacket. Burning. He beat his hands on the flames on his shoulder. He screamed something that wasn't words and dropped himself to the ground and rolled and rolled and rolled until at last he'd put out the flames in his clothing.

I ran to the spot where he lay. Babcock appeared at my side. The man was lying face down. Together, we rolled him over.

We were staring into the face of Meyer Tate.

The shoulder had burnt off his jacket, and the skin underneath looked like scorched meat. He stared up at us from the ground, babbling some sound like a strangled duck.

"If you try to get away," Babcock said, "I'll sit on your shoulder."

The back side of the house was a huge wall of fire. And I thought, Goodey's inside.

I ran to the front door. Smoke was pouring out at the top. I ducked down low where the air was still good and ran hunched over into the front room. The fire was in the back wall and spreading to the roof. I was protected from the heat by the kitchen wall. But I had to stay out of the smoke. I got down on my hands and knees and crawled to the side bedroom. Goodey was on the bed in his sleeping bag, curled up on his side. I was afraid to stand up, so I tugged on the sleeping bag — and it wouldn't budge. I poked at Goodey — but he wouldn't wake up. I braced my feet on the bed and tugged again — and the sleeping bag, with Damon Goodey inside, tumbled off the bed and on top of me on the floor. He started thrashing in the sleeping bag. I wiggled out from under him.

"Get out!" I shouted. "The house is on fire!"

For a moment he sat there in his sleeping bag,

looking totally confused. Then it clicked. He looked at me. He smelled the smoke. He stood up.

"Get down!" I shouted. "Don't breathe the smoke!"

He ducked.

Together, on hands and knees, we crawled out of the house. As soon as we were out the door, Danny met me and grabbed my hand. He pulled me up. Goodey stood up and ran toward the lake.

"You're a *fool*," Danny said. "You could've been *killed*."

"No," I said. "I made it."

"You could've let him *burn*," Danny said. "Nobody'd *mind*. Whose side are you on?"

"Our side," I said.

"What side is *that*?"

"House rules."

Danny looked at me as if I were speaking in Latin or something, which didn't surprise me because I wasn't sure what I meant, either. All I knew for sure was that I'd had to rescue him. And I'd do it again. Because that's who I am and what I stand for.

In the distance, I heard sirens.

Suddenly, I wondered: Where was Flake? Why wasn't he here? Was he in the flames? Had he caught himself on fire and run away?

I looked all around.

Then I heard a yowl. A scratching sound. From the barrel.

I peered inside.

Sure enough, there was Flake. Wet and unburnt.

Looking, in fact, quite pleased with himself.

We lost the next day's soccer game. We were too sleepy, and they were too fast.

Danny's house was a total loss.

My mother found a mobile home that was going to be vacated in a month. It was located behind a farmhouse a little ways out of town, not far from the quarry where Danny's father sometimes worked.

"I'm afraid it needs a little fixing up," she said.

"That won't bother us," Danny said.

When Danny's father called from Oklahoma, Danny told him about the fire and about the mobile home.

His father said he'd come back. He said there was nobody he knew in Oklahoma anymore.

I'd like to say that Damon Goodey was so grateful to me for saving his life that he shook my hand and promised to be my friend and protector for the rest of his days. But he didn't. The next time I saw him he just stared at me. At least, though, he didn't throw any rocks.

Meyer Tate confessed from his hospital bed that he'd set all the fires. The sheriff charged him with arson and insurance fraud, but since all the structures had belonged to him and no people had been hurt — except for Tate himself — nobody expected him to go to jail.

"But why would he set fire to his own garage?" I asked my father.

"So people wouldn't suspect him."

"Was he trying to frame you?"

"I don't think he cared to frame me, personally, but he wanted to put somebody under suspicion, and I always happened to be the one who was around. He could probably see me walking around at night from his house. He's got the view."

"So he did it just for the money?"

"Yes. And now the insurance company wants it all back. And he'll have to pay a fine. He'll be bankrupt, even if he stays out of jail."

"What does bankrupt mean?"

"It means you have no money. It means you have debts you can't pay off. It means he won't be building any new houses."

Or tearing down any more old ones. Good news.

I still owed him a dime.

"Dad?" I said. "When I talked to Meyer Tate, he said he thought you were an honorable man."

"I thought *he* was, too," my father said. "I guess at least one of us was wrong." Then he smiled his wry smile.

"He said he saw no profit in having you in jail. Then he set fire to his garage. I think he wanted to show that you were innocent."

"Maybe. And also, he offered that reward when I was in jail."

Then my father got a funny look on his face, and said he had to make a phone call to the sheriff. He went into his study and closed the door.

When he came out, he said, "Boone, that reward money was posted as a bond. Tate can't take it back. The money's still there. And it belongs to the three boys who captured the arsonist: you, and Danny, and Babcock."

So Meyer Tate had to pay a reward for his own capture, and pay it to the people who captured him.

At dinner we were all celebrating and laughing, and Flake was diving into a bowl of cornflakes, and we were trying to explain the whole situation to Clover and Dale, who simply couldn't get it. Clover was saying, "What? Who? How come? Why do people . . . Why don't they just . . . Why doesn't everybody . . ." Then she closed her eyes and shook her head and said, "Why, why, why?"

I looked at her in confusion and realized that it was the same question I'd been asking myself so often lately. Each time the words were different. But the question was always the same. And the answer, I knew, would be a long time coming for me as well as for Clover. Right now, there was only one way I could respond.

I looked at Clover. I winked my eye.

"Dsh," was all I could say.

Danny wanted to blow the money on radio-controlled cars and video games and all the things he'd always wanted but could never buy.

Babcock said we should save the money for college.

I said we should replace the Trashathon money that Emma stole. Then the team could still go to Australia. Except, I wanted my fifty-two dollars and ninety cents back. For my dirt bike.

"Hey! I want a dirt bike, too," Danny said.

We'd been walking as we talked, and now we were at the side of the lake. The goose was honking at us from the water, while Flake was barking at the goose from the shore. It was a standoff.

Babcock stood at the edge of the water while Danny and I argued. I said that I'd donated the fifty-two dollars, so I should get it back regardless of what happened to the rest of the money. Danny said I'd offered it as a reward and that he was entitled to his share of it just as he was entitled to his share of the rest of the reward. I said, "What did you do to deserve the reward anyway? It was my dog that caught him."

Danny said, "It was my oil drum that saved your dog from burning up."

I said, "It was my idea to follow my father."

Danny said, "It was my house that he burned. We couldn't've caught him if he hadn't had a house to set on fire."

"Does it matter?" Babcock said. He was standing with his hand outstretched. A dragonfly rested shimmering on his finger. "Does it really matter?" he said softly.

Danny and I each took a step toward Babcock, and the dragonfly lifted off of his finger and hovered a few feet above our heads, flashing in the sun like an emerald with wings.

"G-a-a-a-awd," Danny said. "Can you teach me how to make them come to my finger?"

Babcock — calm, quiet, steady — studied Danny, who was fidgety, jumpy, jerky.

"I can try," Babcock said.

He held out his hand again and moved his lips, making no sound that I could hear. The dragonfly hovered lower, lower, until again it came to Babcock's finger — alighted, but not at rest — quivering with life.

I could see Danny wanted to step over to where Babcock was standing, but also he was afraid to move for fear of scaring the dragonfly away.

Flake waded into the water. The goose retreated, still honking. Somewhere in the distance I could hear the sound of carpenters hammering, building a house. Behind me was the shell of an abandoned car.

Another dragonfly — orange, like fire — sparkled past my eyes with a rustle of wings. Out over the pond, I could see dozens more.

I had to agree with Babcock. What's the importance — does it really matter? We could each do what we wanted with the money — or, more likely, what our parents wanted. The argument seemed so very small while the world seemed so very large.

Danny and I tried to imitate Babcock. Silently we

moved our lips. Gently we reached out our hands. We were in the house of the dragonflies, learning the rules. Three friends, for better or worse, awaiting the next adventure in the expanding universe of rocky planets and brilliant stars, we stood in the sunlight, speaking to dragonflies.

About the Author

Joe Cottonwood lives in a small town in the Santa Cruz Mountains of California. He is forty-two years old, has been married for twenty years, and has three children. He makes his living repairing and remodeling houses as a licensed general contractor. For relaxation, he makes bread.

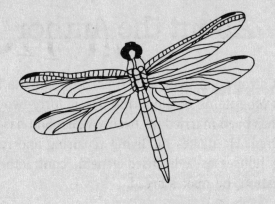

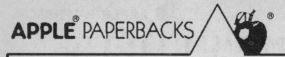

APPLE® PAPERBACKS

Pick an Apple and Polish Off Some Great Reading!

BEST-SELLING APPLE TITLES

❏ MT43944-8	**Afternoon of the Elves** Janet Taylor Lisle	**$2.75**
❏ MT43109-9	**Boys Are Yucko** Anna Grossnickle Hines	**$2.75**
❏ MT43473-X	**The Broccoli Tapes** Jan Slepian	**$2.95**
❏ MT42709-1	**Christina's Ghost** Betty Ren Wright	**$2.75**
❏ MT43461-6	**The Dollhouse Murders** Betty Ren Wright	**$2.75**
❏ MT43444-6	**Ghosts Beneath Our Feet** Betty Ren Wright	**$2.75**
❏ MT44351-8	**Help! I'm a Prisoner in the Library** Eth Clifford	**$2.75**
❏ MT44567-7	**Leah's Song** Eth Clifford	**$2.75**
❏ MT43618-X	**Me and Katie (The Pest)** Ann M. Martin	**$2.75**
❏ MT41529-8	**My Sister, The Creep** Candice F. Ransom	**$2.75**
❏ MT42883-7	**Sixth Grade Can Really Kill You** Barthe DeClements	**$2.75**
❏ MT40409-1	**Sixth Grade Secrets** Louis Sachar	**$2.75**
❏ MT42882-9	**Sixth Grade Sleepover** Eve Bunting	**$2.75**
❏ MT41732-0	**Too Many Murphys** Colleen O'Shaughnessy McKenna	**$2.75**

Available wherever you buy books, or use this order form.

Scholastic Inc., P.O. Box 7502, 2931 East McCarty Street, Jefferson City, MO 65102

Please send me the books I have checked above. I am enclosing $_____ (please add $2.00 to cover shipping and handling). Send check or money order — no cash or C.O.D.s please.

Name _____

Address _____

City_____ **State/Zip** _____

Please allow four to six weeks for delivery. Offer good in the U.S.A. only. Sorry, mail orders are not available to residents of Canada. Prices subject to change.

APP591